MW00851765

The Life Story of

By Iris Allen

written by
MARK WAID & BRIAN AUGUSTYN

art by
GIL KANE, JOE STATON & TOM PALMER

lettered by
GASPAR SALADINO

colored by
LOVERN KINDZIERSKI

separations by
DIGITAL CHAMELEON

cover painting by
GLEN ORBIK

DC COMICS
NEW YORK, NY

THE LIFE STORY OF THE FLASH.
Published by DC Comics.

DC Comics, 1700 Broadway, New York, NY 10019.
A division of Warner Bros. - A Time Warner Entertainment Company.
Printed in Canada.
First Printing.
Publication designed by Eddie Ortiz.

TABLE OF CONTENTS

INHERIT THE WIND

BARRY HENRY ALLEN, ONE OF TWINS, was born in the small town of Fallville, Iowa on May 13th to Dr. Henry Allen and his wife, Nora. It was a late birth, and tricky; the power was out at Fallville General.

Lightning had struck the building.

Barry grew up an only child in so many ways. He was never told about his sibling, never learned the truth about him. Instead, he embraced the lonely solitude that life in a tiny farm town brought. With no neighborhood boys his age to keep him company, he found his one true friend in, of all things...the pages of a comic book.

From almost before he could read, Barry collected comics, rabidly fascinated by tales of high adventure that couldn't help but electrify the life of a little boy raised in East Nowhere. He followed many different series, but his favorite was the one based on the adventures of a real-life hero from a generation past. With the help of his mother, Barry donned the costume of his idol, the Flash, and fought as much crime as an eight-year old was likely to find in Fallville, Iowa.

Barry wasn't completely alone in his fantasies. Aiding and abetting with all her budding thespian skills was Barry's own little damsel in distress, a girl named Daphne Dean. Daphne, as far as anyone in her hometown would ever know, would fifteen years and two Academy Awards later become Fallville's most famous native. All her life, Daphne carried a torch for Barry that could have thawed the polar ice cap, and all his life, Barry was mostly oblivious to the ferocity of her crush. To his mind, their relationship lacked that which was most important to him: chemistry.

That was Barry's other passion. A lot of farm-belt boys grow up to be agricultural wizards, but Barry went a step beyond. He spent most of his teenage years experimenting on the soil from his aunt's corn acreage, and it's no coincidence that her crop won blue ribbons at the county festival for the rest of Barry's life.

Barry's interest in science wasn't simply a product of that farmtown mentality. His room was always neat, his toys were always put away, everything had a place. I suspect that, instinctively, he sensed something important, something secret, was missing from his family and his life, and if he let the world get too cluttered, he'd never find it. Above all else, Barry craved order and certainty, and that's precisely what chemistry provided him. Every molecule of every element patterned out just so under his microscope, every mathematical equation calculated precisely from the tip of his pencil. He couldn't tolerate anything that disrupted his sense of harmony.

There was only one aspect of Barry's life that was in eternal tumult, one that he could have learned to control...

...if the boy had ever learned how to read a watch.
FALLVILLE COUNTY FAIR
WRAP 'N PAK

--AND IF THOSE ARE ALL THE ENTRIES IN THE AGRICULTURAL COMPETITION, GENTLEMEN, WE CAN BEGIN AWARDING--
GARDEN
NOT ALL THE ENTRIES, JUDGE. HERE COMES ALLEN, JUST UNDER THE WIRE.
AS USUAL.

EXCELLENT WORK, ALLEN! IN FACT, WE'RE AWARDING YOU--
HAVE YOU SEEN CINDY?
SHE SAID SHE'D MEET ME AT SEVEN... IT'S ONLY A LITTLE PAST THAT... WHERE...?

AS I WAS SAYING, YOUR ENTRY JUST EARNED YOU AN AGRICULTURAL SCHOLARSHIP TO SUN CITY UNIVERSITY, MR. ALLEN.
OH.
THEY'LL BE GLAD TO SEE SOME-ONE AS BRIGHT AS YOU.

TRY TO SHOW UP BEFORE YOU GRADUATE.

Barry made it to Sun City U almost in time to get half the courses he wanted.

He stuck it out, however, graduating summa cum laude in only three years, majoring in organic chemistry while minoring...

I WAS JUST LUCKY TO STUMBLE ONTO THE CRIME SCENE, PETE. SAW SOME SOIL SAMPLES THAT COULD BE TRACED TO A SPECIFIC AREA.
NICE. YOU EVER THINK ABOUT BEING A COP FOR REAL?
DON'T ANSWER THAT YET. NOT UNTIL YOU READ THE JOB OFFER THEY MADE YOU.

WHO?

THE CENTRAL CITY POLICE. SPECIFICALLY, THE SCIENTIFIC DETECTION BUREAU.

FORGET IT, ALLEN. DOW, WAYNETECH AND LEXCORP ARE OFFERING MUCH BIGGER BUCKS FOR EASIER JOBS. WHO WANTS TO BE IN LAW ENFORCEMENT?

CENTRAL CITY, HUH...?

FLASH

It's likely Barry would have become a policeman despite his fannish urging. His moral gyroscope was already oriented in the general direction of helpfulness, and nothing irritated his sense of order more than the chaos of the criminal mind. Barry never really admitted how much his desire to be like the Flash influenced his career decision, but in the end, it didn't matter. He devoted his life to a cause that fulfilled him. Everyone should be so lucky.

After finding an apartment big enough to accommodate a backroom laboratory (Barry never could stand being separated from his Bunsen burners for more than a few hours at a time), he moved to Central City.

Which is where I came in.

THUNDERSTRUCK

I KNEW THE STORY WASN'T TRUE, and it haunted me all my life.

According to the family records, I was Iris Ann West. My birth parents, so the story went, were Nadine West and her husband Ira, one of the most brilliant physicists of this or any age. Ira holds degrees from the most prestigious universities in the world. Unfortunately, he can't remember where he keeps any of them.

I was the last of their three children. The oldest, Robert Rudolph, liked football, cars, and terrorizing younger kids out of their lunch money. The next, Charlotte, played housewife with the neighbor boy Edgar Rhodes from the time she was five until she was thirty-two. Every day with these strangers made me feel like our sibling connection was a freak accident. At night, I dreamed I was really adopted, abandoned by parents I never knew.

Truer words. But I wouldn't learn that for years to come.

Still, even as a little girl, I'd always suspected something was fishy about my upbringing. That's why I grew up digging for the truth. Award-winning reporter for the high school paper. Columbia graduate, with a brief internship at the Daily Planet. Never any doubt in my mind as to my mission in life; investigative journalism was the only career I ever considered. Secrets unveiled, mysteries revealed; that was my motto. I wanted to be the next Cronkite, the next Lane, the next Bernstein. I wanted to belong in their ranks.

I wanted to belong somewhere.

After college, Daddy's patent royalties started me on a trip around the world. Once I turned in exclusive photos on the Markovian Riots, freelance assignments took me the rest of the way, twice. Along the way, I saw justice served and injustice done. I witnessed the human heart in action and saw all the things a camera could never capture. And I never lacked for companionship; I dated rich rajahs who knew no English, cute princes who thought my Nikon stole their souls. I turned down at least three marriage proposals from men who wanted me to settle down. But even if I'd wanted to settle down, I couldn't have. I was still searching for someplace to be.

Eventually, even I needed a break from the world tour. I promised myself a year back home and, fooling myself into thinking I was slumming, I settled down at Central City's Picture News, a prestigious daily tabloid light on the text and heavy on the snapshots. And as a young woman in an exciting town, I dived head-first into the dating pool...

...and hit my head on a very shallow bottom.

The irony is staggering. Embarrassingly enough, the news game is crawling with people who dig everywhere but into their own souls. So many of the men I met were utterly superficial, more concerned with the pedigree of their suits than the righting of wrongs around them. Their idea of "advocacy journalism" was penning a movie review.

I tried like hell to date within my species, but anchormen were a bore, radio broadcasters clammed up, and print journalists never shut up. And no matter where we went on dates, these egocentric men were forever jockeying for attention, more focused on themselves than on the world around them. To my growing disappointment, the men of Central City were no more interested in getting to the truth than they were in buying throw pillows.

Still, I was in a comfortable place as a single girl. Even for my time, I was a pretty progressive thinker; women who believed they had to find a man in order to be happy sent me into orbit. While following the hundredth tip on the thousandth crime story, I finally concluded that there was, frankly, no place in my hectic life for a man who'd probably never be strong enough to put up with me, anyway. I wasn't disappointed, I wasn't heartbroken; I had simply gotten realistic. I was sure I didn't need the electricity of romance.

CENTRAL CITY'S MOST ELIGIBLE?
Iris West, Picture News Photojournalist, seen here with

And then, suddenly...

...lightning struck.
FAASH!

SAY CHEESE, CREWCUT.
HUH...?
IRIS WEST. SWING THAT SEXY LITTLE THING THIS WAY.
THE CAMERA, THAT IS.
P.D.

YOU'RE GONNA NEED MY PICTURE WHEN... OFF THE RECORD... I NAB JACK GIACOMO FOR ICING BOSS VANELLI HERE.
WHEN YOU NAIL HIM? EXCUSE ME, BUT WHO'S THE PRIMARY ON THIS CASE?
IRIS WANTS MY STORY! IT'S FRONT-PAGE STUFF, AND--
UMM... PARDON ME, OFFICERS... I KNOW YOU WANT THIS TO BE A MURDER...
POLICE CRIME

...BUT I'M GOING TO HAVE TO RULE SUICIDE.

WHAT? BUT-- GIACOMO--
--MY CASE--

--CAN'T HINGE ON THIS. POWDER BURNS... PARAFFIN TEST... SOLID EVIDENCE. SORRY, GUYS.
MAYBE VANELLI WANTED TO FINGER GIACOMO ON HIS WAY OUT... BUT HE DID IT SLOPPILY.

ALLENNNN ...WE NEED THIS, MAN! CITY'S BETTER OFF WITH GIACOMO BEHIND BARS... HOWEVER WE GET HIM THERE!
YOU KNOW THAT! HE'S A COP-KILLER, ALLEN!
C'MON...BEND THE EVIDENCE...

SORRY, GUYS. I KNOW GIACOMO'S A MONSTER... BUT I GO BY THE BOOK.
They didn't think I heard, but nothing's louder than an irate cop.
And what was with crewcut?
My job was done. I had a deadline to beat. So why couldn't I leave?

What was I investigating now?
SOME TIE, CREWCUT. PRETTY DARING FASHION STATEMENT.

IT GOES WELL WITH MY POCKET PROTECTOR. I LIKE BOW TIES. LISTEN, MS. WEST, ABOUT THAT PICTURE YOU TOOK...
"How soon will it run?"
"Can I get a 5x7 glossy?"

"Make sure you spell my name right."
...LOSE IT, OKAY?
WHY? YOU IN WITNESS PROTECTION OR SOMETHING? COME ON, OFFICER ALLEN, LET ME USE IT. IT'LL BE A THRILL FOR THE FOLKS BACK HOME.

I'D RATHER YOU NOT.
AND WHY IS THAT?
BECAUSE I'M NOT THE STORY.

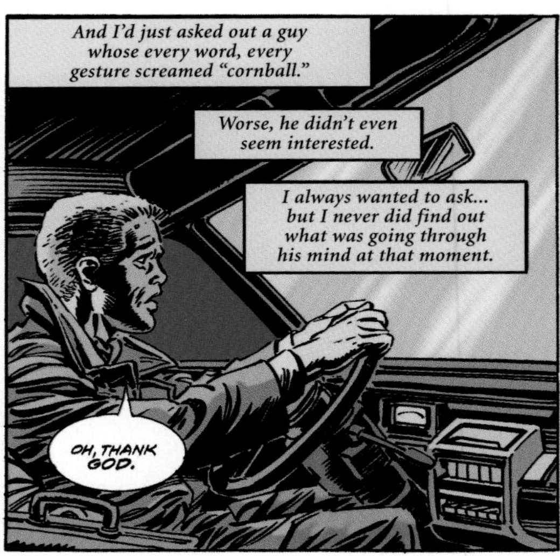

Our first date was at the July 4th picnic in Central City Park. I don't remember what I made for Barry, but I remember packing lots of mayonnaise and white bread.

That was the first time I ever made him laugh.

By sunset, we'd made a promise to come back to that park every year on that anniversary. It was a joke, a promise made in whimsy, but I think we both knew by day's end that there was something more to it. I know I did. I knew what I'd found. There was honesty in the plane of his hand, stability in the grace of his footfalls. In a world obsessed with glitz and image, Barry Allen was the Real Thing.

Bow tie and all.

The more we talked, the more we found in common. We liked the same actors, hated the same movies. We both surrendered ourselves to jazz, and I never thought I'd find anyone my age who liked the Big Bands, but there he was. There were no demands on me when I was with Barry. We just...were.

He teased himself constantly. He told me he was boring, and then proved to be anything but. Even in his quiet moments, his analytical mind was always pushing towards some truth. Only once did I tell him how sexy I thought that was. He immediately coughed an entire lemonade through his nose, so I decided to keep it to myself from then on. But it always stayed true.

Barry was at his most boyish at night, when the lights of Central City pumped their energy into the air. We both loved that city, and that was one of our strongest ties. In it, we could be explorers together, mapping every brick and bulb in town, finding the best restaurants for lunch, the best theaters for plays, the best doorways for a stolen kiss.

STOCKING UP FOR THE WINTER?
JUST... FIGURING ON BEING BORED...
BARRY, YOU'RE ON TIME. IS EVERYTHING ALL RIGHT? ARE YOU OKAY...?

NICE TIE, BY THE WAY. IT IS THE FAIR. YOU CAN GO CASUAL--
--OHHH!
EAT
FRED'S
FROZEN CUSTARD
IT'S MY LUCKY TIE.
COME ON. LET'S GET HIGH.

Coming from crewcut, I knew what that meant.
He was so excited by the ferris wheel, he was positively adorable. Clearly, he wanted to share his enthusiasm.

I didn't have the heart to remind him I'd stood atop Kilimanjaro, so a county fair ride was hardly a...

...thrill...

NICE NIGHT.
LOOKS LIKE RAIN TO ME.
I... HADN'T NOTICED...
YOU... BEAUTIFUL LOOK TONIGHT...

From that night on, we were inseparable. I'd found the one man I knew would never abandon me, who would fight time itself to be by my side, and I wasn't about to let him go. He held no secrets.

A BOLT FROM THE BLUE

I REMEMBER THE FIRST TIME Barry took me to his office. It sounded thrilling. He worked at the Scientific Detection Bureau of the Central City police force under Captain Harvey Paulson, Chief of Detectives and a damn fine interview himself. I envisioned banks of high-tech equipment, detectives racing in and out to crack cases, a constant buzz of kinetic motion. What it was...was a lot of desk work.

...lose track of time.
WHAT'S THIS? "CALL IRIS TONIGHT 6:00 SHARP-OR ELSE!"
UH-OH!

IRIS...

KRA-KOOM!

WELL... SWELL.

=SIGH=
FREAK ACCIDENT...TAKE ME ALL NIGHT TO CLEAN THAT UP. AH, WELL...TACKLE IT AFTER DINNER, I GUESS...
FLASH

LEAST I WASN'T HURT...
TAXI! TAXI!
OH, COME ON... TAXIIII!
TAXI

At first, he thought the accident was playing tricks on his mind.
MAYBE I WAS DREAMING FOR A SECOND. MAYBE... ...MAYBE THE LIGHTNING BLASTED SOME MOPEE ON ME. MAYBE...
OHH-- LOOK OUT!
FLASH

Maybe not.

THE FOOD... IT WASN'T... MOVING, HARDLY...
...BUT THAT'S IMPOSSIBLE. NO... IT WAS FALLING... AND I CAUGHT IT. I WAS THAT FAST. I MOVED AS FAST AS--

FLASH COMICS 10

IRIS!
ROXY

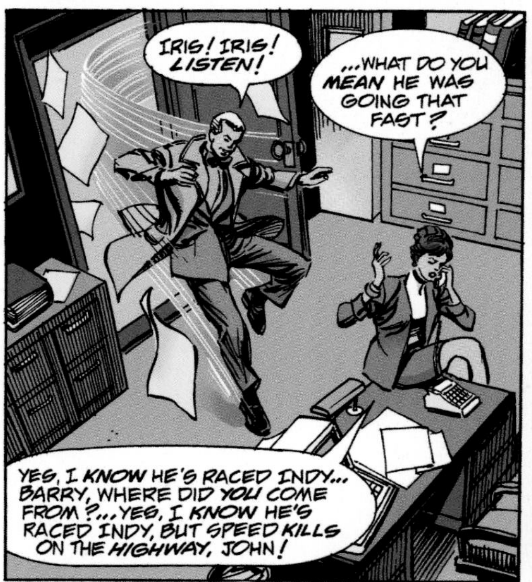
IRIS! IRIS! LISTEN!
...WHAT DO YOU MEAN HE WAS GOING THAT FAST?
YES, I KNOW HE'S RACED INDY... BARRY, WHERE DID YOU COME FROM?... YES, I KNOW HE'S RACED INDY, BUT SPEED KILLS ON THE HIGHWAY, JOHN!

HOW LONG WILL HE BE LAID UP?
TERRIBLE... BUT IT COULD HAVE BEEN WORSE.

I JUST DON'T UNDERSTAND THAT KIND OF BEHAVIOR AT ALL.

NOT ONE BIT.
GOT ANOTHER CALL. GOTTA GO.
WEST HERE. HI, TAYLOR. READY TO--?

WHAT? YOU SAID YOU WERE GIVING ME THE INTERVIEW! TAYLOR, WE'VE ALWAYS HAD A GOOD RELATIONSHIP!
DON'T GIVE ME THAT! YOU KNOW HOW I FEEL ABOUT SURPRISES, TAYLOR!
FINE. FINE!

BAD DAY?
YOU CAN'T IMAGINE. AND... GET THIS... YOU REMEMBER BONNIE?
PICTURE NEWS' OTHER SERIOUS PHOTOG, RIGHT? YOU LOVE HER WORK.
LOVED. SHE JUST GAVE NOTICE. SHE'S DROPPING HARD NEWS FOR AN ASSIGNMENT AT SOME FASHION RAG!

SHE HAD A SURE, SERIOUS CAREER... AND SHE'S RUNNING OFF!
GOD, YOU CAN'T COUNT ON ANYONE IN THIS WORLD TO DO WHAT THEY SHOULD... TO STAY WHERE THEY BELONG!

LISTEN TO ME GRIPE. I'M SORRY. I JUST... MAYBE THAT'S WHY I LOVE YOU SO MUCH, BARRY. YOU'RE NORMAL AND YOU'RE SURE AND YOU'RE STABLE. YOU'RE MY ROCK.
I KNOW YOU'LL ALWAYS BE THE SAME BARRY I FELL FOR.
NOW... WHAT WERE YOU GOING TO SAY?

THAT I LOVE YOU.
AND THAT NOTHING WILL EVER CHANGE BETWEEN US.
NOTHING.

And he left without another word.
Today, when I think back, I still want to be angry. I just wish I knew with who.
Because I ranted and raved...because he took it to heart... he kept secret from me the most marvelous thing that had ever happened to him.

But that's the way Barry was, I know that now. Whenever he felt a fear he couldn't handle...

...he decided to mask it.

LIFE IN THE FAST LANE

IN TRIBUTE TO HIS BOYHOOD HERO, Barry adopted the Flash identity for himself, if in name only. Out of deference, he chose an entirely new look to go along with the role. Ever self-effacing, Barry worried that duplicating the senior speedster's outfit was too presumptuous, too disrespectful. Thus, Barry crafted his own, distinct, and—to my way of thinking—sexier uniform.

Packing weeks into seconds, he tailored a costume out of the experimental fabric he had developed while in college and found a way to store it secretly and safely. His ring, which, before I learned his secret, had a different origin every time I asked him about it in an off-guard moment ("It's a school ring." "It's from a police fraternity." "My dad gave it to me."), contained a secret compartment and a special mechanism that drove the hydrogen atoms out of the fabric, miniaturizing it, allowing it to fit miraculously inside the ring. When released to the air, however...

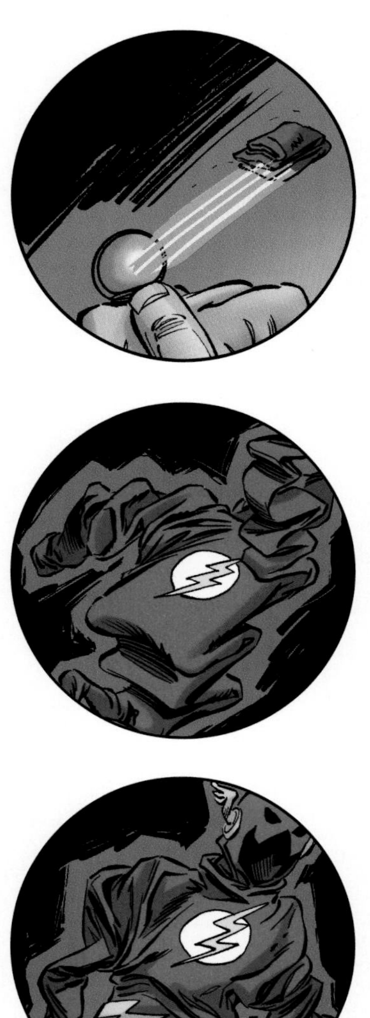

Without breaking a sweat, the slowest man alive could suddenly outrace a beam of light, rocket across the ocean like a skipping stone...

...laugh at gravity...

...and pluck bullets out of the air as if they were summer plums.

He could saw through solid objects like a straw hurricaned through an oak tree...
...or ghost through them by vibrating his molecules at unique hyperfrequencies.

Finally, he could run as far and as fast as he'd ever dreamed of running. Nothing could stop him, no one could catch him.
Almost no one.
FLASH!

FLASH!

HEY, FLEETFEET!

I WANT TO TALK TO YOU!

And that was pretty much our work relationship, at least until he got his act down a bit more firmly. Until then, he always sounded like he had a cold. In retrospect, he was trying way too hard.

For about a week, the Flash was the most outrageous character Central City had ever seen. Then someone, somewhere, decided to turn up the heat. Weird characters began oozing out onto the sidewalks. First came the turtlenecks...

Before long, Central City would become a mecca for costumed criminals of all shapes and sizes. So would the world, for that matter. But Flash didn't have to fight them all alone.

Soon, super-heroes were popping up all over the place. In California, a man calling himself Green Lantern fought crime with a magic ring and an iron will. Aquaman and Martian Manhunter—one from the deep sea, one from deep space—began making headlines, as did Star City's Black Canary. And just as the previous Flash had done, Barry chose to work with his contemporaries, forming a team. They called themselves the Justice League of America, after the old Justice Society, and Barry secretly hoped that the attendant hoopla might bring his predecessor out of his mysterious retirement. It didn't.

Flash made friends outside the JLA, as well. One of them exemplified the word "flamboyant." The Elongated Man was longer on charm and detective skill than he was on ego, but just barely; he was the first super-hero to shout his real name from the rooftops. Realizing he had no interest in fitting in with the secret identity crowd, he abandoned his mask about eight seconds after he first donned it. Ralph Dibny wanted everyone to know that he was, as he always put it, "the World-Famous Elongated Man."

Still, Barry's best friend, costume or no costume, was Green Lantern. Their rock-solid relationship puzzled me from the start; Green Lantern was a reckless hotshot, while Barry was methodical and pensive. It took them a while to adjust to one another's ways, but once they did, they were an extraordinary twosome.

Within a year, Central City's politicos found a way to honor their new favorite son. A bond drive established the Flash Museum, a non-profit attraction that made Flash's eyes go wide every time he thought about it. Barry conned me into calling in sick on opening day, and we were there for four hours. Sometimes, for a reporter, I wasn't very astute.

The museum stands to this day, supervised by an elderly Shakespearean actor named Dexter Myles who's a show in and of himself. Barry himself had a hard time believing his own adventures when Dexter would recount them in full stentorian tone, but that sweet old man remembers details about Flash's cases that even I've long forgotten.

There were magazine covers and documentaries and parades...and, oh, the fan clubs. Kids all across the nation had found their new idol. Early on, *Picture News* did a fluff piece on the surge in signups for junior high school track teams. In one of those rare moments when Flash stood still, we caught him reading the report. He was grinning from ear to ear.

Letters were pouring in so quickly, even Flash had a tough time keeping up with them, but he replied to every single note, making more friends and more fans with each "sincerely." Every kid in America wanted to meet him, shake his hand, race him.

Only one got his wish.

LIGHTNING STRIKES TWICE

WALLACE RUDOLPH WEST, a boy from a wide place in the road known as Blue Valley, Nebraska, may well be the star of the greatest rags-to-riches tale I've ever heard. I know his story intimately. We're family.

Wally was the only child of my thuggish brother, Rudy. Rudy nurtured his wife, Mary, and his son the same way a woodpecker nourishes a tree. He chipped away and chipped away at his family until they were too cowed to stand tall before him. Chalk it up to his dysfunctional relationship with our dad; Rudy demanded from them the love he never seemed to get from Ira, and he demanded it hard and in a very loud voice.

Wally's letters and phone calls, and there were many, broke my heart. He'd always seen in me someone very much like himself, someone who clearly didn't belong in the baboon cage and knew it. He looked to me for guidance, which put me in a tough spot. I didn't have the right to interfere with Rudy's parenting, but I'd sooner have died than see Wally suffer. Fortunately, Rudy and Mary played into my hands beautifully during Wally's tenth summer.

They sent him to stay with me.

Wally was beside himself with excitement, and as much as I'd have loved to believe it was because of me, he was supercharged because he knew Central City was the home of the Flash, and Barry had no greater, more devoted follower. Wally was proud of saying that he was the president of the Blue Valley Flash Fan Club. He thought I didn't know he *was* the Blue Valley Flash Fan Club. I played along. This is the job of an aunt.

By the time Wally came to visit, Flash had been operating for about a year, twelve months in which he'd become an even bigger celebrity. Wally's dream was to meet him. Since we'd already established how comfortable Flash was around me, I went to my next best hope. I prayed that Barry, with his police connections, might be able to set up some sort of meeting. Had I only known then what I was asking....

Barry made no promises. He simply took Wally for an afternoon during which Wally learned a lot of things. He learned that Barry didn't actually carry a gun. He learned that Barry didn't patrol the streets. He learned that, God bless him, Barry was about as exciting to a ten-year-old as a case of the mumps.

And then he learned what it was like to have a dream come true.

I HAVE A SURPRISE FOR YOU. FLASH USES MY BACK ROOM LAB SOMETIMES. HE SAID HE'D DROP BY AROUND NOW.
YOU'RE HIS FRIEND? WHY WOULD HE HANG AROUND WITH...
I MEAN... YOU KNOW THE FLASH? HE'S HERE?
GO SEE.
WALLY, IS IT?
HELLO, WALLY.
GHU... GHU... GHAH...
WE HAVE A LOT TO TALK ABOUT. ANY QUESTIONS?
HOW... HOW'D YOU GET TO BE SO FAST?
FAIR ENOUGH. I WAS STANDING IN FRONT OF A CHEMICAL CABINET JUST LIKE THAT ONE...
...WHEN, WITHOUT WARNING, A LIGHTNING BOLT BURST THROUGH THE WINDOW, COVERING ME WITH ELECTRIFIED CHEMICALS.
FROM THAT MOMENT, I WAS SUPER-CHARGED!
I WISH SOMETHING LIKE THAT WOULD HAPPEN TO ME...
=HA HA= SORRY, WALLY. YOU KNOW WHAT THEY SAY. LIGHTNING NEVER STRIKES TWICE IN THE SAME--

KA-BLAM
WALLY!
And yet, it did. Called down from the heavens by fate or coincidence or the power of a little boy's most passionate wish, it created a second speedster that day.
As big on secret identities as Barry was, of course, it should come as no shock that he masked Wally, as well.
Irony of ironies, then, I was the one who gave him his handle. One Picture News headline later, he was "Kid Flash." Wally finally had the father figure he deserved.
Barry couldn't have been happier. He finally had someone to share his experiences with. Someone who recognized the staccato thunder of Mach 5 footfalls, who knew the hot sting that came from catching a bullet.
Wally was dead-set on the code name "Speedy," but some bowslinging teenager in California had that one sewn up.
They were great together.

They were linked in another way, as well. Though neither of them knew for sure quite yet, they both suspected there was more to Wally's incredible accident than could be explained by even the most elastic chance. Only after Wally became an adult would he learn more about exactly what happened that afternoon.

Wally spent the next few months trying to get me to drop Barry Allen and start dating the Flash. He didn't knock it off until the following summer, when Barry finally revealed to Wally the secret of his dual identity. Like before, of course, they made a pact to tell me nothing. Once I finally found out, Wally was deeply ashamed he'd kept so much from me. I let him off the hook. He's not the one I blamed.

The following summer, lightning struck once more. An accident with a matter-transforming machine gave substance to one of Flash's idle notions, transforming Wally's original outfit into a new design with which Flash had been toying. It was arguably the best-looking super-hero costume anyone had ever seen, at least as far as teenagers' suits went, and Wally wore it with pride for years and years, until he traded up and back.

But I'm getting ahead of myself.

THEIR COMMON THREAD belonged, appropriately enough, to a tailor. His name was Paul Gambi. He made a nice side living outfitting the costumed lunatics who came to Central City, for theirs was an unending parade.

The first major criminal to battle Flash was Captain Cold, a two-bit thug who turned a miniature stolen cyclotron into a gun capable of projecting ice and reducing temperatures to absolute zero. Oddly enough, for someone so frigid, his crimes were often crimes of passion; for a while, every time he popped up, it was to win the heart of some young debutante he'd opted to stalk. At least once, he set his sights on me, but Flash froze him out.

Cold's sometime-ally was Heat Wave, an asbestos-clad pyro who used flames the way Cold used snow and sleet. One of the first of Barry's enemies to reform, Heat Wave stumbled onto the secret of Barry's dual identity but never used it to his advantage, thank God. In later years, he actually considered himself Barry's friend, and Barry, God bless him, tried hard to overlook their past relationship.

The Mirror Master used reflective surfaces to commit his crimes. As limiting as that sounds, it made him a master of illusion, gave him access to other dimensions, and enabled him to create any number of laser- and light-based weapons.

Captain Boomerang was an Australian brought to our shores as part of—of all things—a toy company sales blitz. The toymakers, none too bright, had no idea they'd hired as their spokesman a mercenary with a scientific bent, one who could turn a simple throwing stick into a deadly assault device.

Despite their colorful outfits and grand schemes, a good number of Barry's enemies were small-timers who built their m.o.'s around props and gimmicks. One of the least of their number was the Top, who spun around Central City emulating the child's toy after which he'd named himself, obviously more for kicks than out of any tendencies towards criminal genius.

Conversely, Barry was genuinely challenged by the Trickster, a circus aerialist who invented, among other things, antigravity shoes that allowed him to walk through the air. Trickster's stock-in-trade was his arsenal of baleful gags: exploding rubber chickens, poisonous dart guns, cream pies laced with ether. As hard as it is to imagine someone like that giving the Flash much trouble, trust me: the Trickster was far more dangerous than he appeared, especially given his not-incidental skills as a consummate con man.

Only by moving faster than sound was Barry able to defeat the Pied Piper, who used sonics to control the minds of others. Privately, Barry and I used to wonder how accepted he would have been by Central City's other tough-talking, macho super-criminals had they realized that the Piper was secretly gay. Since those days, of course, he's come out and, fully reformed, enjoys a new life as a research scientist with his boyfriend, James.

One of Barry's strangest foes was Mr. Element...or should I say Dr. Alchemy? Cursed with a split personality, Al Desmond constantly shuttled back and forth between two identities, leaving Barry to wonder which he'd face during any given battle: Element, whose ray gun conjured substances out of thin air, or Alchemy, whose Philosopher's Stone could transmute inanimate objects up and down the periodic table.

The Weather Wizard had the same origin as too many of these psychos; he was a two-bit loser who stumbled across a super-scientific device which gave him mastery over some deadly force. The dumb luck of criminals in Central City, along with all the loose locks on the city's R&D labs, used to drive Barry insane. Whenever the Wizard was on the loose, Barry used to stay up nights praying that he'd never get smart enough to use his weather-manipulation rod to its fullest extent. Fortunately for Mother Earth, the Wizard stuck to robbing banks rather than wrecking Earth's ecosystem. Frankly, that shortsighted "ambition" was, more than anything else, what began to bond these criminals together into a loose organization. Calling themselves the Rogues Gallery, they teamed up mostly to make Barry's life as miserable as possible; plundering jewelry stores and art galleries seemed simply part of the gig, a competition to see which of them could give Flash the biggest runaround.

Not everyone was allowed to play their little reindeer games. On occasion, villains far more clever and more deadly than any mere Rogue blew into town, and the tamer criminals kept their distance. One of them was amazingly bright for someone who dragged his knuckles on the ground, and his name was Gorilla Grodd.

Grodd, a refugee from an entire city of super-intelligent gorillas hidden deep in the heart of Africa, plagued Barry not only with his savage strength but with the mental powers of telepathy, telekinesis, and hypnotism that Grodd collectively referred to as his "force of mind." Grodd wasn't interested in knocking over banks, except perhaps literally. He would settle for nothing less than complete world domination.

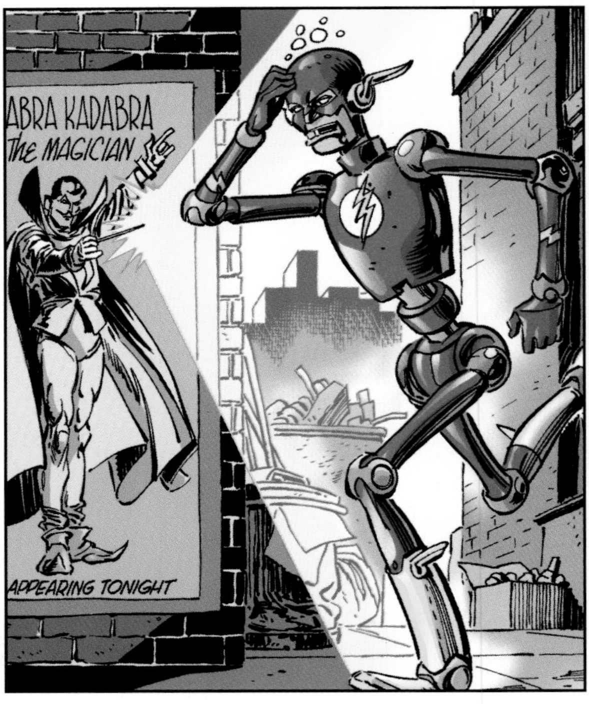

Neither was the mad magician Abra Kadabra ever accepted as one of the Rogues. They rightfully shied away from a man who could, on a spasmodic whim, transform them into plants or polliwogs. A terrorist and agent of chaos in his home era of the 64th century, Kadabra—reports vary—either left for or was exiled to our time, where he made a name for himself by using malevolent technology so beyond our understanding that it appeared to be magic.

Kadabra gave Barry a tougher time than most. The twinkle in his eye wasn't cleverness. It was insanity. Desperate for attention, for applause, for validation, Kadabra always turned his attacks into elaborate productions, full of sound and light and chilling unpredictability. That said, he still set his sights abominably low. He could have killed Barry. Instead, he turned him into a puppet, or a hunk of sidewalk, or tinkered with his speed. Like all the others, he was, in the end, a little light in the homicidal tendencies department. More meddlesome than threatening, they were all relatively benign, all petty.

Except one.

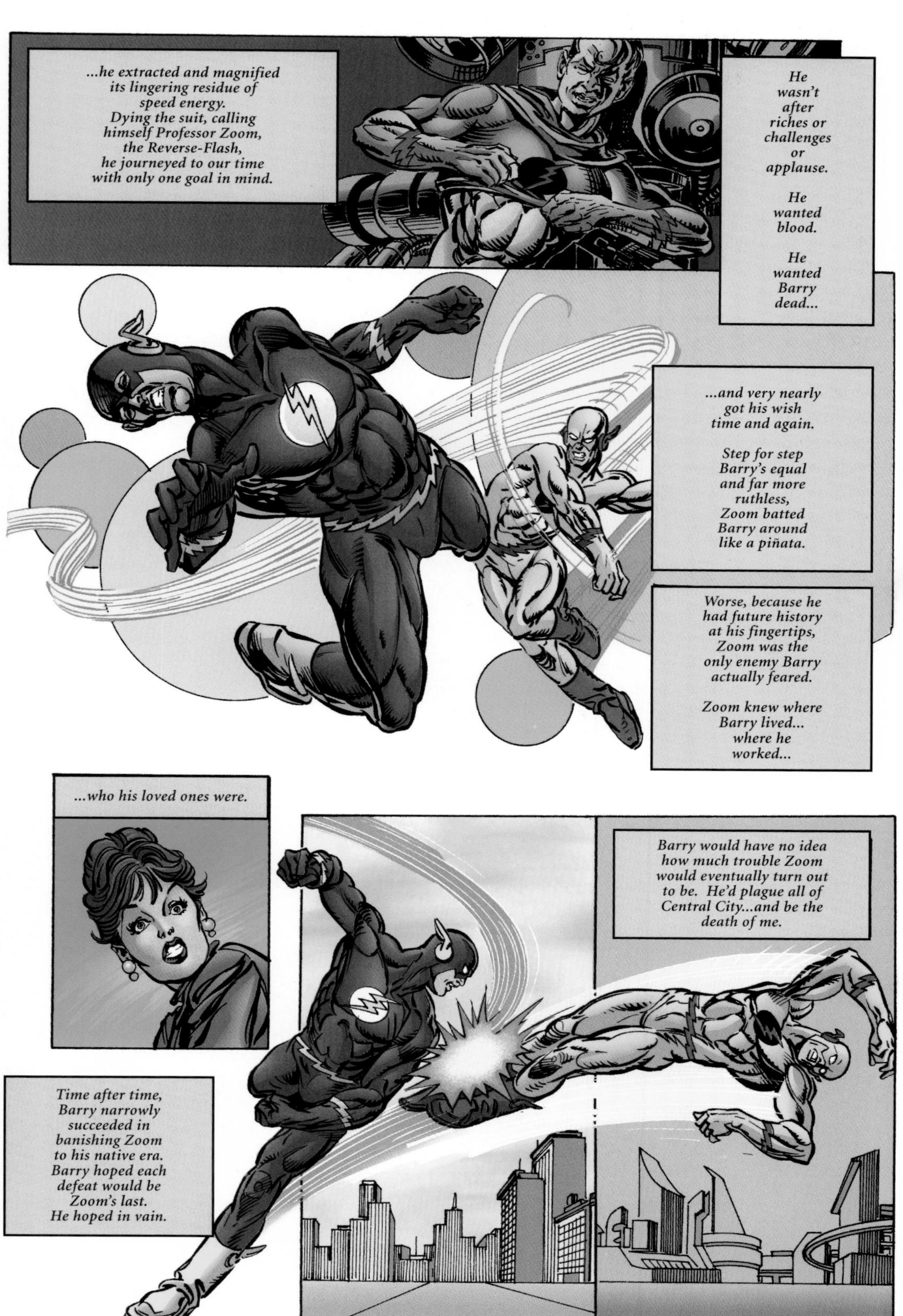
...he extracted and magnified its lingering residue of speed energy. Dying the suit, calling himself Professor Zoom, the Reverse-Flash, he journeyed to our time with only one goal in mind.
He wasn't after riches or challenges or applause.
He wanted blood.
He wanted Barry dead...
...and very nearly got his wish time and again.
Step for step Barry's equal and far more ruthless, Zoom batted Barry around like a piñata.
Worse, because he had future history at his fingertips, Zoom was the only enemy Barry actually feared.
Zoom knew where Barry lived... where he worked...
...who his loved ones were.
Barry would have no idea how much trouble Zoom would eventually turn out to be. He'd plague all of Central City...and be the death of me.
Time after time, Barry narrowly succeeded in banishing Zoom to his native era. Barry hoped each defeat would be Zoom's last. He hoped in vain.

STOLEN THUNDER

ALL BARRY WANTED was a tip of the hat.

By now, the whole world knew him as the Flash. News agencies billed him as the one and only, fans referred to him as the Fastest Man Alive. As far as they were concerned, he owed nothing to anybody. And yet, the greater the Flash's fame grew, the more uncomfortable he was in the role, the more embarrassed he seemed by the identity. For a time, though practically no one noticed, he even stopped referring to himself explicitly as "The Flash," sidestepping the name altogether whenever possible. He knew it wasn't truly his.

No one was sure into what ether Barry's forerunner, the original Flash, had slipped. Like Judge Crater, like Amelia Earhart, the speedster of the 1940s had simply vanished one day, so abruptly that even those who cared—and there were fewer every generation—began to doubt that he'd ever existed.

The new Flash held no such doubt. At first, an elated and hopeful Barry took every sky-streak of lightning, every sonic boom, as a sign that the "real" Scarlet Speedster was returning in a crash of thunder to once more reclaim the spotlight. But as Barry's first months became a year, as he fast began to replace his predecessor in the hearts and minds of the public, hope began to turn to dread. Suppose, Barry feared, that the first Flash did return? Though they'd never met, Barry felt he owed him so much...and even if he had any idea how to go about giving something back to him, stealing his thunder without permission, without approval, wasn't the way to do it.

Barry often suspected that the mystery of Jay's disappearance had something to do with the infamous Bridge to Nowhere. It seems odd now that a city the size of ours had built such a bridge, and odder still that no one wondered why. But as long as anyone could remember, we'd looked across the river to see nothing and were never disappointed.

There were stories, of course. Fairy tales of a great sister city that once gleamed across the water. But no one believed fairy tales...
...any more than they believed a man could move faster than the wind.
Still, SOMETHING called to those sensitive enough to hear...

WEIRD. WHEN I VIBRATE AT A CERTAIN FREQUENCY, I DETECT A SOUND... A HARMONIC TONE, ALMOST... COMING FROM...

...ACROSS THE BRIDGE...?

He was stunned. Maintaining a specific internal frequency, Flash found an entire city vibrating out of synch with the rest of the world...

...its citizens sleepwalking through its streets, frozen in time.

A yellowed newspaper did little to allay the shock. Flash had chanced upon Keystone City, home of the original Flash.
KEYSTONE CITY HERALD
CITY IN CHAOS!
WHERE IS THE FLASH?
Suddenly, he remembered. Keystone was Central City's sister. Everyone knew that...but someone had caused the world to forget it with a simple soundwave. And if Flash was going to find out who...
...he was going to need help.
JAY! JAY GARRICK! WAKE UP!
I'VE SEARCHED THE WHOLE CITY FOR YOU!
WAKE UP! HOW COULD WE HAVE BEEN MADE TO FORGET AN ENTIRE TOWN? WHO COULD HAVE PULLED OFF SOMETHING LIKE THAT?
AGAIN WITH THE VIOLIN SCREECHING, FIDDLER? I CAN'T HEAR MYSELF THINK OVER THAT GROTESQUE RACKET!
THAT "RACKET" IS ART, THINKER, YOU PHILISTINE-- PRODUCT OF THE SAME MUSICAL GENIUS--

--THAT CREATED A RESONATOR TO VIBRATE THE ENTIRE CITY OUT OF REAL SPACE--LULLING ITS CITIZENS TO SLEEP, LEAVING KEYSTONE OURS TO PLUNDER!
YOU BUILT IT, FIDDLER, BUT I DESIGNED IT, AND SHADE THOUGHT IT UP, YOU FREAKISH--
GENTLEMEN, PLEASE... NO BICKERING. WE HAVE A PROBLEM. FOR THE FIRST TIME IN YEARS, I SAW SOMETHING REMARKABLY FLASH-LIKE RUNNING THROUGH THE STREETS. IF OUR OLD FRIEND IS INDEED AWAKE--

--LET'S LURE HIM TO HIS DOOM ONCE AND FOR ALL--AND TAKE THIS NUMBER ON THE ROAD!

The villains went on a rampage, ready for final battle. The Thinker calculated the odds at three to one.
K-CHANG!

He thought wrong.

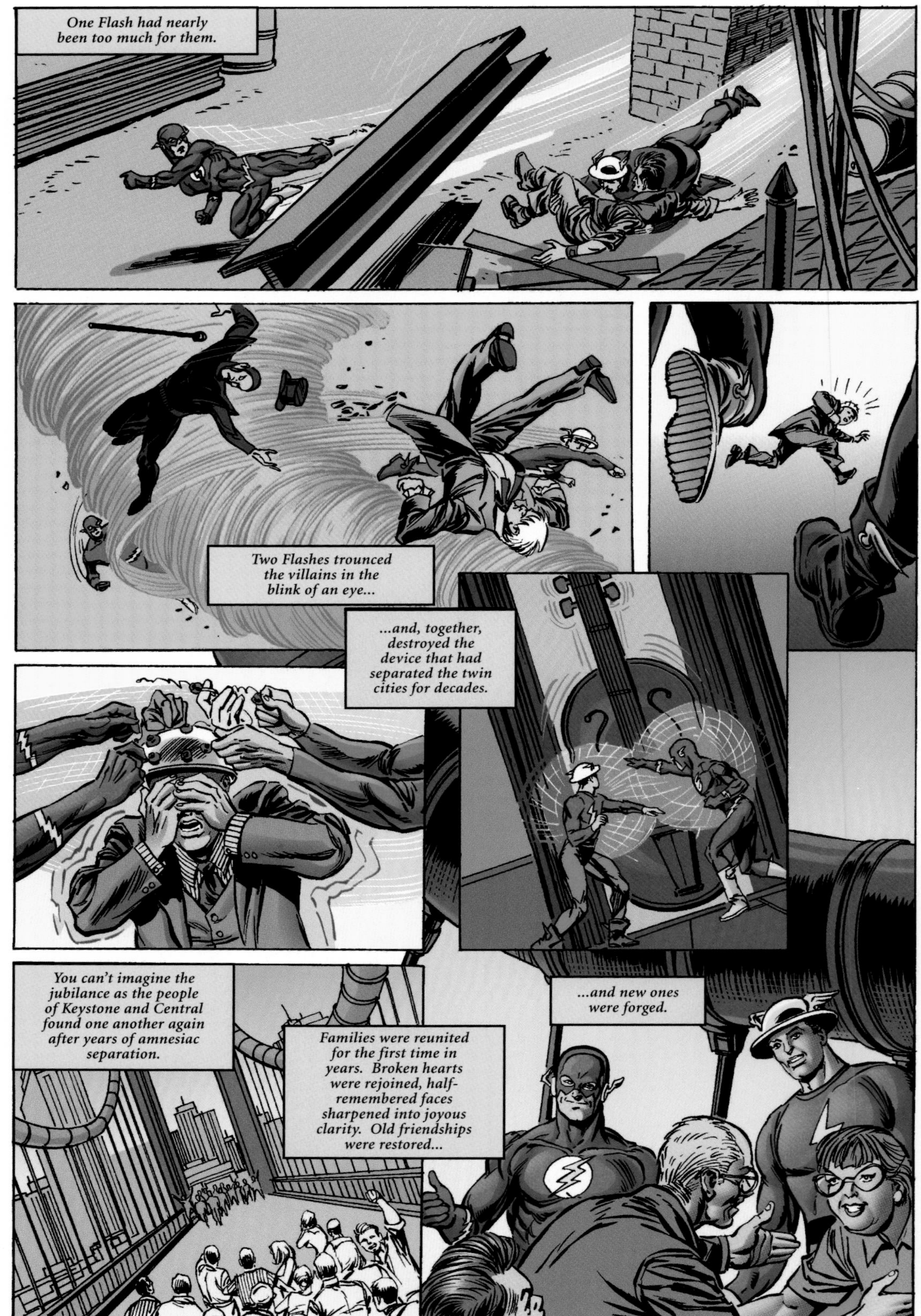
One Flash had nearly been too much for them.
Two Flashes trounced the villains in the blink of an eye...
...and, together, destroyed the device that had separated the twin cities for decades.
You can't imagine the jubilance as the people of Keystone and Central found one another again after years of amnesiac separation.
Families were reunited for the first time in years. Broken hearts were rejoined, half-remembered faces sharpened into joyous clarity. Old friendships were restored...
...and new ones were forged.

The Flashes spent a week that afternoon exchanging information.
...NAME'S JAY GARRICK, ALL RIGHT. GOT MY POWERS BY INHALING SOME VIBRATIONALLY CHARGED FUMES.
YOU SAY YOU KNOW ALL THAT FROM READING A FUNNYBOOK?
YES, SIR. I'M...KIND OF A FAN...
HAPPENS. ME, I READ THE PULP MAGAZINES WHEN I WAS A BOY. "WHIP WHIRLWIND"...NOW, HIS ADVENTURES WERE DOWN-RIGHT THRILLING...
THIS YOUR PLACE?
FLASH MUSEUM
UMM... IN A MANNER OF SPEAKING...
NICE CLIPPINGS. LOOKS TO ME LIKE YOU'VE DONE ALL RIGHT BY THE FLASH NAME, JUNIOR. WHY DON'T YOU KEEP ON USING IT?
ME? BUT--
SON, MY CREAKY OLD BONES WERE READY FOR A REST EVEN BEFORE THE FIDDLER AND HIS CRONIES CAME ALONG. BESIDES, FOR WHAT YOU DID TODAY, I'M IN YOUR DEBT. YOU REALLY WANT THE ROLE, TAKE IT...
...WITH MY BLESSING.
THE FLASH
THE JOB IS YOURS.
RUN WITH IT.

'TIL DEATH DO US PART

WE HAD EVERYTHING GOING FOR US, Barry and I. As our wedding day approached, we glowed with happiness and anticipation. The faith, the trust I had in my husband-to-be was immeasurable, for I knew beyond every shadow of a doubt that in a world full of betrayal and confusion, he would always keep his promises. In fact, he proved me right on our wedding night.

And when he did, he nearly destroyed our marriage.

He made his vow a few weeks before the big date, at the end of one of his adventures. Through the machinations of an alien race, his identity had been revealed to the world at large, and no one was more stunned than I. In years to come, of course, our nephew Wally would prove that it was possible for a hero to operate fully well without a secret identity, but in those days, among Barry and his peers especially, it was considered a job requirement. Terrified that criminals might strike at his family and loved ones, Barry eventually found a way around the disclosure. Through some time-travel manipulation that I'll be the first to confess I never understood, he managed to turn back the clock and erase the world's knowledge of his dual identity... but not before I made him vow to tell me anew on our wedding day rather than keep it secret from his wife. I knew he'd be as good as his word. After all...he promised.

I'm not proud to say that it wasn't the last time I tried to extort a vow out of him. Two weeks later, I pressed him hard on what I thought was something else altogether...and I still feel guilty to this day.

The Vanelli/Giacomo gang war had erupted, and every policeman in Central City felt the heat. Officers were working double and triple shifts to protect the public, which put a huge number of cops on the street—a huge number of targets.

BARRY... THERE'S NOTHING YOU COULD HAVE DONE.

THEY WERE FRIENDS OF MINE, IRIS. VANELLI'S MEN CUT THEM DOWN LIKE WHEAT.
AND FLASH BROUGHT VANELLI TO JUSTICE.

COLD COMFORT TO SOME.
I KNOW. I CAN'T IMAGINE WHAT IT WOULD BE LIKE TO BE A POLICEMAN'S WIFE.

BUT I'M--
I KNOW YOU ARE. AND YOU EARNED A DESK JOB. AND WHEN I SEE THIS, BARRY, I CAN'T TELL YOU HOW GRATEFUL I AM FOR THAT.

TO THINK OF YOU OUT ON THE STREETS... YOUR LIFE AT RISK EVERY MOMENT OF EVERY DAY... I...
...I JUST DON'T THINK I COULD HANDLE IT.
PROMISE ME, BARRY. PROMISE ME YOU'LL STAY AT THE DESK.

I'LL DO MY JOB.

September brought a fairy tale wedding in the truest sense-complete with a blackhearted villain and a damsel in distress. Though I wouldn't find out until years later, Professor Zoom meddled with the ceremony, almost stole my hand in marriage by momentarily impersonating Barry, and nearly killed the Flash...all, as usual, too quickly for we mere mortals to perceive. Besides that, it was rather uneventful...

...other than the moment my dad asked Barry about grandkids.

I DON'T... I MEAN, WE'VE NEVER... WE...

HA, HA! RELAX, MY BOY! BUT DON'T WAIT TOO LONG! MY DAUGHTER'S GOING TO MAKE A HECK OF A MOTHER HERSELF SOME-DAY!

YES, SIR. YES, SHE IS.

That night, I watched Barry sleep while I lay awake dreaming of all our tomorrows.

He seemed restless...troubled. I'd never known him to talk in his sleep, but that night, he couldn't shut himself up.

Clearly, he had something on his mind, and when I realized what it was...

ZOOM...stay AWAY...! He's... after IRIS...

He'll HURT her... he WILL...because he KNOWS...

... I was dumbfounded.

...knows that BARRY ALLEN... is the FLASH!

It would have been simple to dismiss it as a nightmare, but I knew better. The moment I heard those words, they unlocked my memories of the last time I'd found out.
I'd known before... and now I knew again.
My husband was the fastest man alive, he was a costumed crimefighter with a dual life. And worst of all...

...he was a liar.
'MORNING, MRS. ALLEN! SLEEP OKAY?
FOR A WHILE.
GOOD. YOU'LL WANT YOUR REST... BECAUSE I HAVE A SURPRISE FOR YOU.
OH, THANK GOD. SOMETHING YOU WANT TO TELL ME, I HOPE?
CAN'T WAIT TO. I'VE BEEN KEEPING SOMETHING FROM YOU, SWEETHEART, BUT IT'S TIME I CAME CLEAN.

TOMORROW, WE'RE TAKING A HONEYMOON CRUISE TO JAMAICA!
...
WHAT?

A... CRUISE. ISN'T THAT... KIND OF SLOW?
SLOW AND STEADY. BUT THAT'S ME, ALL THE WAY, RIGHT?

RIGHT?
Wrong.
Instant vertigo. A whirling emptiness turned my life inside out in an eyeblink.
I wanted to bark at him that not all of us are used to the world suddenly moving at that speed, but I held my tongue and fought to process this non-information.

I was a mess. What should have been the happiest weeks of our lives instead became a mutual torture. I played coy, pretended not to know, and tried to concentrate on the parts of our union that worked...and there were many. Besides, I told myself, I was responsible for this mess.

Or was I? With every passing day, I felt a resentment build. Yes, I'd pressed my husband...but didn't he trust me? Didn't he have faith in me to understand what I'd gotten into, what the risks really were? Didn't I have a right to my own fears? Didn't I have a right to be proud of Barry, as well? My career, my whole life, was a quest for the truth. I knew deep down I shouldn't have to live with a secret.

The strain showed. We weren't as glib as we'd been, we weren't as carefree. Our friends began to worry for us. My father—yes, even my obtuse father had noticed our tension—was constantly after us to get counseling, but neither of us wanted to face the real problem.

I loved my husband...but I wasn't sure I could live with him.

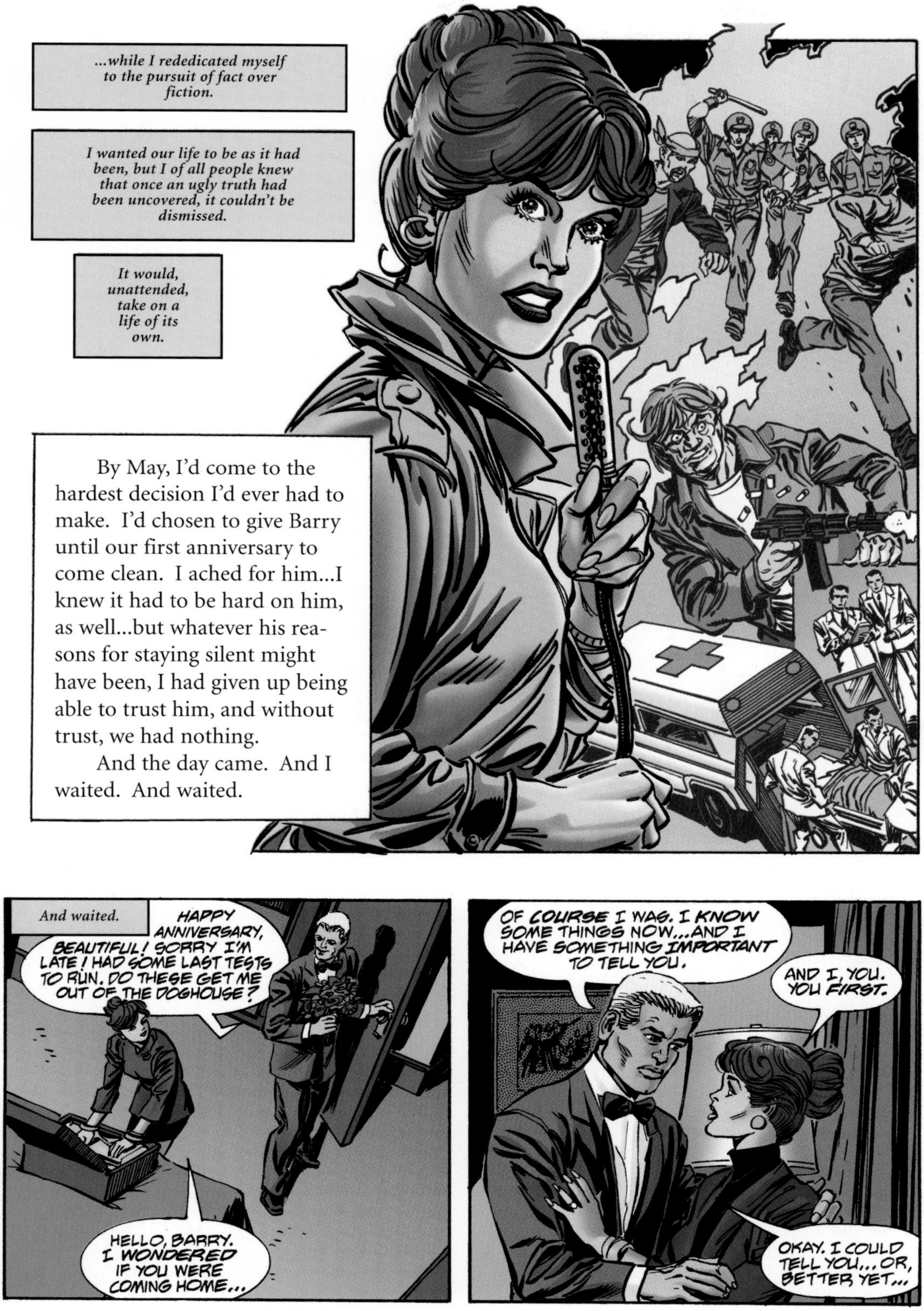

...while I rededicated myself to the pursuit of fact over fiction.

I wanted our life to be as it had been, but I of all people knew that once an ugly truth had been uncovered, it couldn't be dismissed.

It would, unattended, take on a life of its own.

By May, I'd come to the hardest decision I'd ever had to make. I'd chosen to give Barry until our first anniversary to come clean. I ached for him...I knew it had to be hard on him, as well...but whatever his reasons for staying silent might have been, I had given up being able to trust him, and without trust, we had nothing.

And the day came. And I waited. And waited.

...I
COULD
SHOW
YOU!
IRIS, YOUR HUSBAND IS REALLY--
--THE FLASH.
I KNOW, BARRY. I'VE KNOWN FOR A YEAR.
YOU...YOU HAVE? BUT HOW...?
He asked, I answered. I could finally let go everything I'd been holding inside.
I'd been waiting twelve months to be angry at him, and when that rage finally spilled out, it shocked even me.
YOU TALK IN YOUR SLEEP!
I'VE KNOWN ALL THIS TIME! YOU SWORE YOU'D TELL ME ON OUR WEDDING DAY, AND THAT WAS HOW YOU DID IT!
AND I'VE KNOWN, AND I FEEL STUPID, AND HELP-LESS, AND DISTANT, AND LIED TO, AND--
IRIS... IRIS, I... OH, GOD... I'M SO SORRY, AND EMBAR-RASSED, AND--
YOU'RE EMBARRASSED? YOU'RE EMBARRASSED? CAN YOU IMAGINE WHAT IT'S LIKE TO KNOW AND NOT BE ABLE TO SAY?
TO PLAY STUPID WHEN THE FLASH HAS HIS LIFE THREATENED BY HEAT WAVE OR KADABRA? TO PRETEND NOT TO CARE?
TO WONDER WHAT ELSE YOU'RE CAPABLE OF KEEPING FROM ME? TO--
IRIS... I HAD MY REASONS. THEY MIGHT NOT HAVE BEEN GOOD ONES, BUT I...

I KNOW. I KNOW WHY YOU DIDN'T SAY ANYTHING. I KNOW IT WAS BECAUSE OF--
--BECAUSE OF THE KIDS.
WHAT?
YOUR FATHER SAID IT ON OUR WEDDING DAY. HE WANTED TO KNOW WHEN WE WERE HAVING CHILDREN.
AND I REALIZED FOR THE FIRST TIME, IN THAT MOMENT, THAT... I DIDN'T KNOW IF WE COULD.
I HADN'T EVEN THOUGHT ABOUT IT... NOT SINCE I BECAME THE FLASH...
...AND I'D LET YOU MARRY ME ANYWAY.

ALL THESE THINGS I CAN DO, IRIS, ALL THESE POWERS... THEY'RE AMAZING, AND THEY'RE WONDERFUL, BUT THEY'RE NOT NATURAL.
THEY'VE ... CHANGED ME. A HUMAN BODY CAN'T DO WHAT MINE CAN UNLESS IT HAS BEEN TRANSFORMED... AND I OWED IT TO BOTH OF US TO FIND OUT JUST HOW MUCH.
THAT'S WHY I'VE BEEN WORKING SO HARD AT THE LAB. I'VE BEEN RUNNING TESTS.

AND...?
AND WHEREVER THIS POWER COMES FROM... SOMEWHERE OUT THERE SOME-WHERE... IT HASN'T...
...IT HASN'T MADE ME ANY LESS HUMAN...

AND IF IT TURNED OUT THAT WE COULDN'T HAVE CHILDREN?
I'VE SEEN HOW YOU ARE AROUND WALLY. YOU LOVE KIDS.
I COULDN'T HAVE HELD ONTO YOU.
THE HELL. YOU COULDN'T HAVE.

WE HAVE LOTS TO TALK ABOUT, BARRY ALLEN. NO MORE UNILATERAL DECISIONS. NO MORE SECRETS. NO MORE HIDING.
MY HAND TO GOD. I LOVE YOU, IRIS, WITH ALL MY HEART. I'D NEVER DO ANYTHING TO HURT YOU.
SO... YOU WANT TO HAVE KIDS?

SOMEDAY.
GOOD ANSWER... BECAUSE WE SHOULDN'T BE IN A RUSH. WE CAN... BUT THERE'S A CHANCE THEY'LL INHERIT MY POWERS... AND YOU'RE NOT READY TO DIAPER A TORNADO.
SOMEDAY, SCIENCE WILL BE ADVANCED ENOUGH TO COPE WITH SUPER-SPEED INFANTS... BUT UNTIL THEN, LET'S SETTLE FOR LOVING EACH OTHER INSTEAD. DEAL?

DEAL.

FLASH FORWARD

THE SECOND YEAR OF OUR MARRIAGE, like every year thereafter, was easier, more relaxed...and, unlike most couples', more passionate. Now that we finally knew one another, really knew, we found each other's rhythms effortlessly. And while being the secret wife of the Flash carried its attendant frustrations...

...it also had its moments.

THIS IS GOING TO STAIN! BARRY, WE NEED SELTZER! A LITTLE HELP HERE?
BARRY...?

GLADLY, GINA. AFTER ALL, IRIS AND I ARE A TEAM.
RIGHT, HONEY?
Absolutely.

Truth to tell, we kind of kept to ourselves as a married couple. It's not that we were antisocial...
...SO THEN...GET THIS... HEAT WAVE ACTUALLY STARTS TO CRY.
THAT IS SO LIKE HIM...
...we just didn't have a lot to share with other couples.

This wasn't to say that we were hermits. One of our closest friends was Detective Charlie Conwell, an acquaintance of Barry's from the force. Robust and always good-natured, Charlie was well-loved and excellent company. As a widower who didn't know a pot from a spatula, he was welcome at the dinner tables of half the people in Central and spent at least one night a week at our house. I wish it could have been more.

Unfortunately, Charlie's gift for making friends was matched by his gift for making enemies, at least among the underworld. While mounting a shoo-in campaign for the office of District Attorney, Charlie was assassinated, and the city mourned his loss even as it lauded Flash for bringing in Charlie's killers.

Charlie hadn't left our lives completely, though. In tribute to our long friendship, we accepted his daughter Stacy into our home during her first year at Central State University. Though it meant Barry had to be extra-careful not to tip his dual identity, we came to love Stacy almost as if she were our own daughter, and together, the three of us got past our grief. Even after she left, we stayed in touch. She and her husband, Chuck Marston, eventually parlayed their business skills into a successful chain of pizza restaurants whose trademark is, of all things, fast delivery.

I used to kid Barry for having rather eclectic pals, and the neighbor was no exception. He was thirteen. A latchkey kid, Barney Sands shared Barry's fanaticism for old comic books, and the two of them used to gab for hours about their favorite characters and artists. And even if I never understood the difference between a "penciller" and an "inker," I couldn't help smiling whenever I overheard them gassing on and on, God bless them. Barney was an aspiring artist himself. Though both his parents worked—and were, for our money, a little too unattentive—Barry and I tried hard to make Barney somewhat less lonely, and I think we succeeded. Now in his early twenties, Barney's apparently all the rage as the artist of a comic based on the Justice League of America. I know he's happy.

And then there was my father, Ira. We'd never been terribly close; a physicist and a reporter have precious little in common, and as I said before, I never really felt part of the West clan. After my mother passed away, our already-tenuous bond eroded even further. Barry liked him well enough; their scientific conversations were even less comprehensible to me than the comic-book talk. And as incalculably absent-minded as Ira was, he still remembered my birthday. Most years. Oh, I still loved him. How could I not? He was my father...

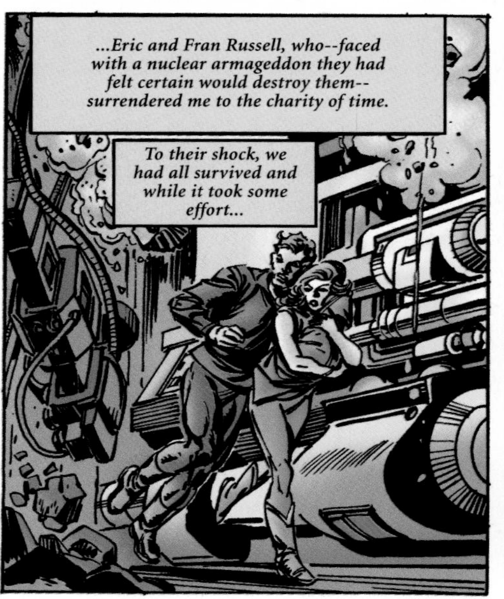

Ira took more doing.
IRIS, THIS IS YOUR FATHER. PLEASE, HONEY, DON'T SHUT ME OUT LIKE...
GO TO HELL.
IRIS, PLEASE. YOU TWO HAVE TO TALK ABOUT THIS. IT'S BEEN WEEKS.
IRIS, WHERE ARE YOU GOING?
IRIS!
NADINE WEST DEVOTED MOTHER
DAMN YOU BOTH. HOW COULD YOU?
ALL THOSE YEARS, YOU LET ME LIVE A LIE. I KNEW IT... I KNEW IT... BUT YOU WOULDN'T ADMIT--
OH!
WHAT AM I DOING HERE? I...I THOUGHT I WAS IN MY LAB...?
I SUPPOSE I AM GETTING FORGETFUL IN MY OLD AGE...
IRIS? IS THAT YOU?
MY DEAR, HEAR ME OUT. IT ISN'T LIKE YOU THINK.
ISN'T IT?

WHY DIDN'T YOU TELL ME I WAS ADOPTED?
DON'T TELL ME YOU DIDN'T REMEMBER!
I WON'T STAND FOR THE MEN IN MY LIFE KEEPING SECRETS FROM ME ANY-MORE. DO YOU UNDER-STAND THAT? DO YOU?
YES.
AND FROM THE BOTTOM OF MY HEART... I APOLOGIZE. IRIS... MY DEAR, DARLING IRIS... DON'T LEAVE ME, TOO.
...
"TOO"?
HOW WELL DID YOU KNOW YOUR MOTHER, IRIS? DO YOU MISS HER LIKE I DO?
DO YOU STILL SMELL HER PERFUME? DO YOU STILL LOOK GOD IN THE EYE AND DEMAND TO KNOW WHY HE TOOK HER AWAY?
RUDY'S NOT THE BEST SON, IRIS... AND CHARLOTTE WAS HER MOTHER'S CHILD. BUT YOU WERE BRIGHT AND SHARP AND FULL OF JOY FROM THE MOMENT I FIRST HELD YOU.
YOU WERE THE DAUGHTER I WANTED, IRIS... BUT I NEVER DESERVED YOU. IT'S NO EXCUSE, IRIS... NONE...
...BUT WHERE YOU CAME FROM...
...IT WAS THE ONE THING I WANTED TO FORGET... AND NEVER COULD.

ZOOM WAS ALWAYS DANGEROUS, but he became Barry's mortal enemy with a flick of his wrist.

I wasn't the only one to whom Barry represented strength and safety. Zoom, the Reverse Flash, seethed with a perverse loyalty all his own. To Zoom, it wasn't enough to be near Barry. He had to supplant him. In fact, during his first and several subsequent trips to the 20th century, Zoom actually went so far as to impersonate Barry and try to steal his life, and though he was always exposed, he was never truly dissuaded. Over the years, Zoom remained fixated on my husband, and time merely fueled his sick obsession. He denied it with every noxious breath, but Zoom either felt or had invented a twisted kinship to Barry that I will forever be at a loss to fully explain. I confess I never realized the depth of Zoom's madness...

DON'T BE FRIGHTENED, DEAR. WHY, I'VE BROUGHT YOU SOMETHING.
AN ULTIMATUM.
I'M TIRED OF ALL THIS RUNNING AROUND. I'VE DECIDED ONCE AND FOR ALL TO PUT YOUR HUSBAND OUT OF MY MISERY.
STARTING TOMORROW, I'M GOING TO WIPE HIM OUT--TAKE EVERYTHING THAT'S HIS--
AND LET YOU--
--BE--
--MY--
--WIFE!
NEVER--!
DON'T DECIDE IN HASTE, MY LOVE. I'LL GIVE YOU 24 HOURS TO THINK IT OVER. BE MINE...OR DIE.
Using some sort of hypno-ray, he erased the threat from my conscious mind so I couldn't warn Barry...
...but he allowed my subconscious to weigh his words. He really was insane if he thought any threat could drive me from Barry's side.

The next night, Barry and I went to a party. Even subconsciously, I knew I was safe despite Zoom's threats. My husband would be at my side. He'd spot Zoom the instant he approached...
...unless Zoom found a way to hide...
...in plain sight.
He'd been spying on us. He knew the theme of the party. "Come as a super-hero or super-villain." How clever.
How damned clever.
IT'S GETTING LATE. SHOULDN'T WE CALL THE SITTER?
WHAT SITTER? WE DON'T HAVE KIDS.
YET.
"YET." SOMETHING YOU'RE READY TO START TALKING ABOUT, MRS. ALLEN?
WHENEVER YOU'RE READY, MR. ALLEN. AREN'T WE A LITTLE OVERDUE...?
YOU KNOW... MAYBE WE ARE...

I'LL GET PUNCH IF YOU SCHMOOZE MY BOSS?
WE'RE A TEAM.
MAY I HAVE THIS DANCE?
YOU!
THREATENED ME! I...I REMEMBER...!
TICK TOCK, SWEETHEART. YOUR TIME IS UP. LOVE ME OR DIE.
NO ONE WILL EVER LOVE YOU, YOU REPUGNANT WORM. NOT EVER. YOU'RE A PSYCHOPATH.
I'D RATHER DIE THAN BREATHE THE STENCH OF A MAN SO CLEARLY BARRY'S INFERIOR.
I...I COULD BE MERCIFUL, IF YOU BEGGED. I COULD SIMPLY DROP YOU INTO THE TIMESTREAM...
HE'D FIND ME. NO MATTER IF YOU LOST ME BY A THOUSAND YEARS, BARRY AND I WOULD FIND ONE ANOTHER...AND HE'D MAKE YOU PAY.
DO YOU... DO YOU REALIZE, MY LOVE, WHAT YOU'RE SAYING...?
YOU'RE THAT DESPERATE FOR HIS ATTENTION? DO YOUR WORST. DO IT NOW. JUST TAKE YOUR FILTHY HANDS OFF ME!
AS YOU WISH. NOT A WORD TO BARRY, THOUGH. I COMMAND IT.
GOODBYE, MY DARLING.

And with that, I was hypnotized again, oblivious to Zoom's vendetta.
His words echoed only once more...
...the split-second he drove his fingers into my brain.
He'd won. Life fled instantly. My last thoughts were of Barry...of the things I wanted to tell him, the things I wanted to hear...
...and of the hatred I felt for the man who stole the life we had planned.
IRIS...?
IRIS!
NO! COME BACK! IRIS, I LOVE YOU!
COME BACK!..
COME BACK...
In time, Barry found my killer. He would have his revenge... but it would cost him dearly.

FASTER THAN LIGHT

FOR ME, THERE WAS NO PAIN. There was only a peaceful consolation that everything I'd heard was true. At the other side of death, there really was a tunnel of light, a conduit to a Heaven beautiful.

RUNNING FROM THE PAST

I WOULD HAVE GIVEN ANYTHING to comfort him.

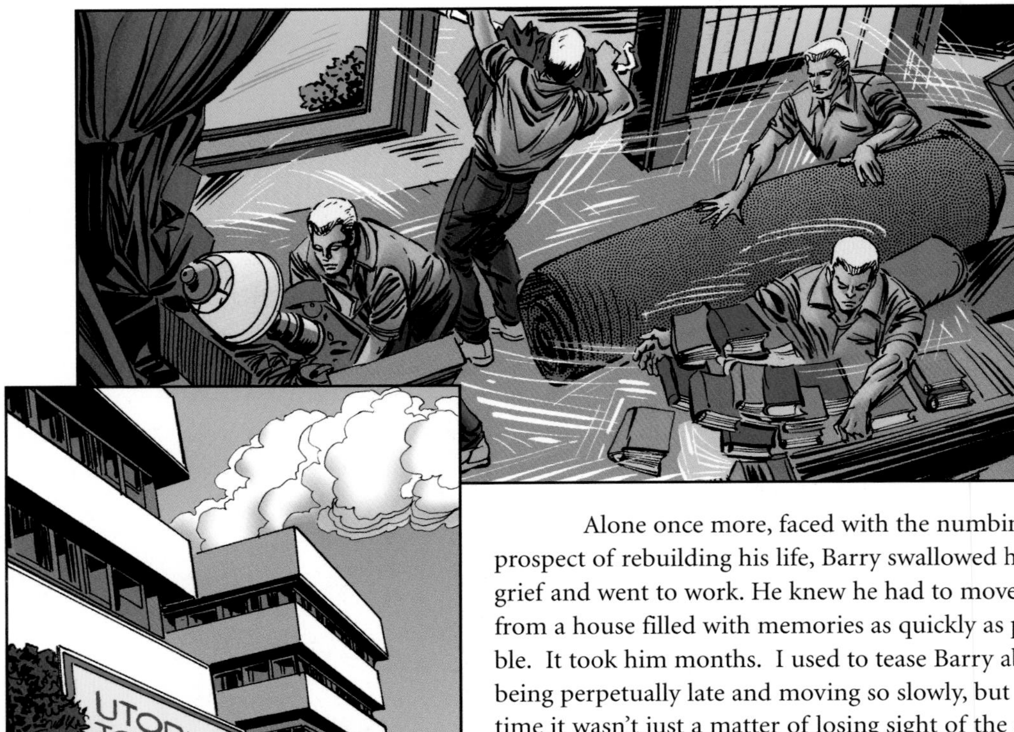

Alone once more, faced with the numbing prospect of rebuilding his life, Barry swallowed his grief and went to work. He knew he had to move away from a house filled with memories as quickly as possible. It took him months. I used to tease Barry about being perpetually late and moving so slowly, but this time it wasn't just a matter of losing sight of the clock.

This time, he needed to linger. At least, that's what I tell myself.

The day the moving van came, Barry shifted into high gear; in fact, maybe into overdrive. He had unpacked his new apartment by the time the movers exited the parking lot and began a rush to fill his new life with new friends. He let his neighbor Mack Nathan, a fellow widower, drag him to every singles bar in Central City, which is an image that both shocks and amuses me. Barry and Mack never got that close; I wonder that the presence of Mack's son, Troy, didn't sadden Barry with remorse over the children we'd never had.

But then, Barry didn't get very close to anyone during the next few months. In an attempt to reestablish some friendships on the force, he spent time with Detective Frank Curtis, an urban-born undercover agent who had little in common with Barry. Barry's boss, Captain Paulson, tried to worm his way into Barry's personal life, but only in order to frame him for the heroin trafficking he himself was secretly heading out of the department. And the less said about Paulson's successor, the punctuality-obsessed Captain Darryl Frye, the better. Suffice it to say that Frye's split-second, time-clock mentality eternally threatened the patience of a man whose wristwatch mocked him every day of his life.

In retrospect, I've come to realize that Barry's frantic scramble to recreate his routine life was doomed to failure from the start. At least, that's what I tell myself. Barry never moved fast, and running a desperate race against his own loneliness so went against his every natural instinct, it clouded his judgment. The friends, the allegiances, even the joys he experienced during this time couldn't help but be transitory.

And then there was his romance.

Fiona Webb was a woman on the run from her own past. Entrenched in the Witness Protection Program, she spent every waking moment in perpetual fear of being discovered by the murderer she'd identified.

I know her heart must have beat faster the moment she laid eyes on Barry; he was the spitting image of the killer. In fact, she was openly hostile, convinced that Barry was out to murder her until, as Flash, he apprehended the true criminal and set her mind at peace. She apologized to Barry with a dinner date and stayed for dessert.

Once she warmed to him, Fiona quickly provided Barry with companionship and the kind of tender attentions that helped soothe the lonely ache that burdened him. To them, forming a relationship was less about creating a new future than leaving their pasts behind. They were never truly in love.

At least, that's what I tell myself.

Inevitably, I suppose, Barry and Fiona's whirlwind romance culminated in a marriage proposal. From the moment the ring went around her finger, the poor girl put all her energy into planning a wedding.
Barry, on the other hand...
...was otherwise occupied.
Zoom was back, and the second he surfaced, Barry abandoned every concern he had save payback.
Every concern.

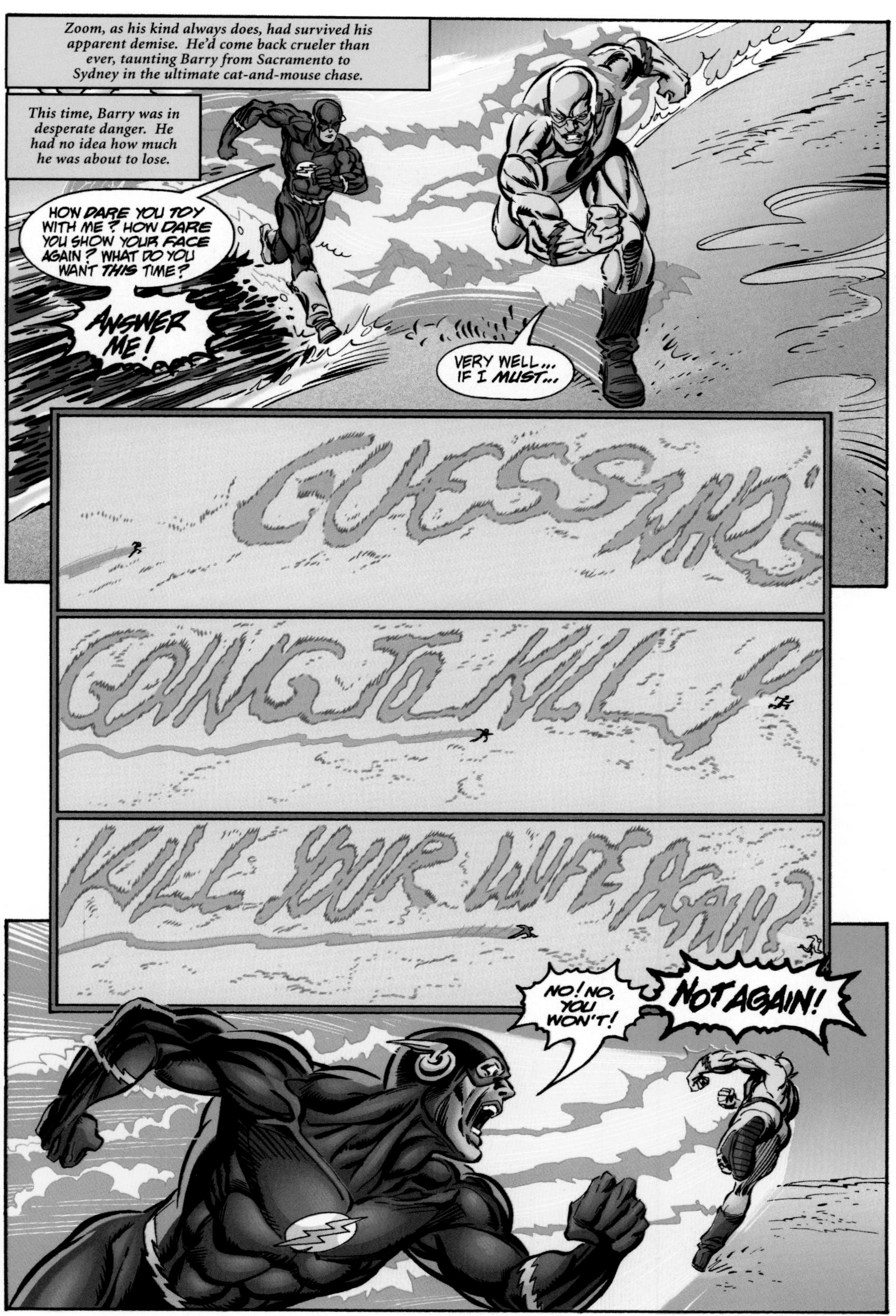
Zoom, as his kind always does, had survived his apparent demise. He'd come back crueler than ever, taunting Barry from Sacramento to Sydney in the ultimate cat-and-mouse chase.
This time, Barry was in desperate danger. He had no idea how much he was about to lose.
HOW DARE YOU TOY WITH ME? HOW DARE YOU SHOW YOUR FACE AGAIN? WHAT DO YOU WANT THIS TIME?
ANSWER ME!
VERY WELL... IF I MUST...
GUESS WHO'S
GOING TO KILL Y
KILL YOUR WIFE AGAIN?
NO! NO, YOU WON'T!
NOT AGAIN!

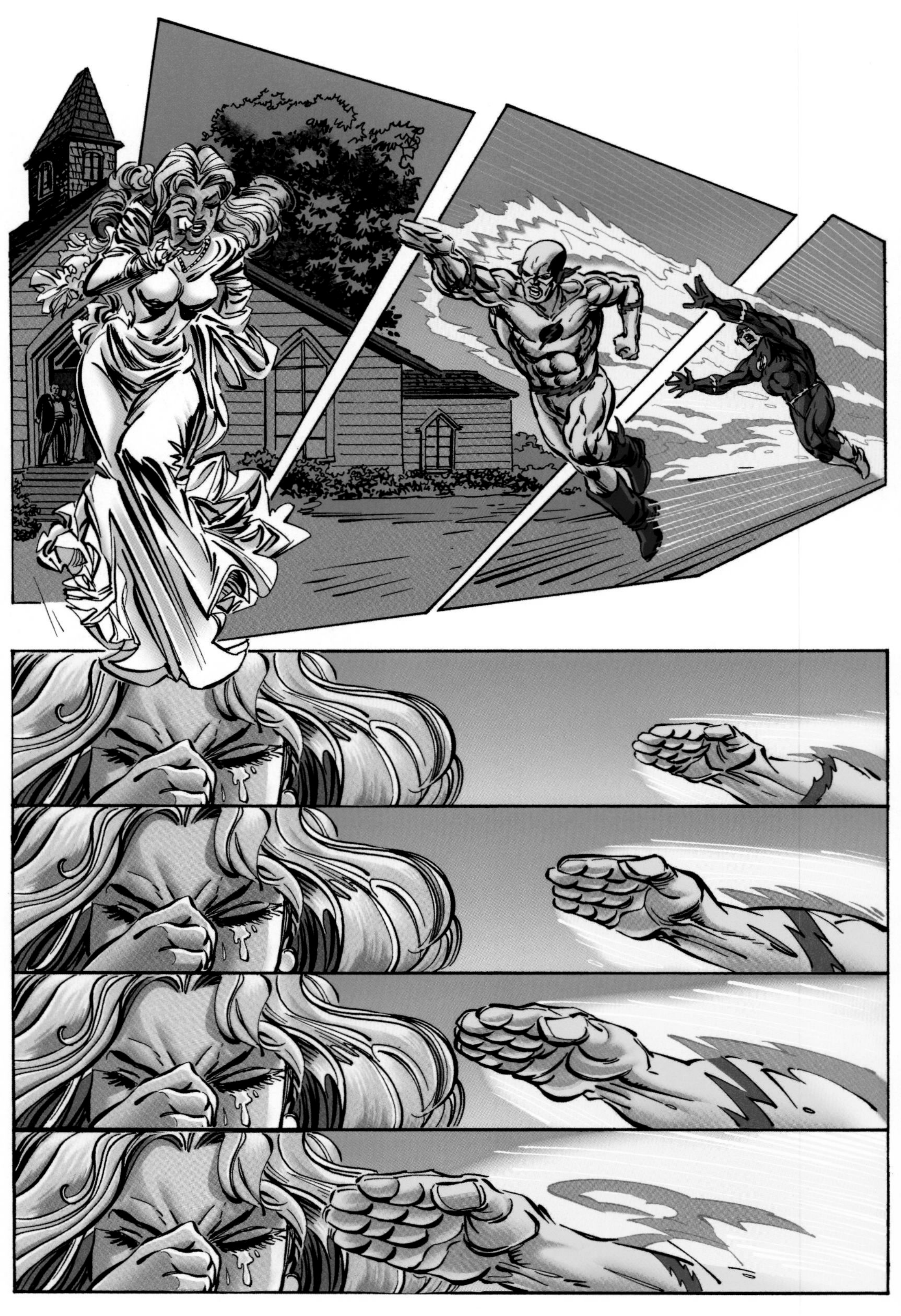

NOT AGAIN!
FIO--
--I MEAN--MISS? ARE YOU ALL RIGHT? I KNOW I STARTLED YOU, BUT I DID WHAT I HAD TO DO TO SAVE YOUR LIFE--
WHAT LIFE? WHAT THE HELL KIND OF LIFE DO I HAVE? WHERE'S BARRY?
BARRY...?
MY FIANCÉ! HE STOOD ME UP AT THE ALTAR! HE DOESN'T LOVE ME! OH, GOD, WHY WOULD HE DO THIS TO ME? WHY?
...
BECAUSE HE CARES FOR YOU! DON'T BE MAD AT HIM. HE'S STANDING RIGHT H--
FLASH? SORRY TO INTERRUPT, BUT--
WHAT? AREN'T YOU KEEPING AN EYE ON ZOOM? FOR GOD'S SAKE, YOU'LL LET HIM GET AWAY!
NOT LIKELY. FLASH... HE'S DEAD.
YOU KILLED HIM.
THAT MEANS YOU'RE UNDER ARREST... FOR MANSLAUGHTER.

THE TRIAL OF THE FLASH

IT WAS ONE OF THOSE TIMES when I was ashamed I'd ever been a reporter. The media frenzy surrounding Barry was unprecedented. No super-hero had ever gone to trial before, certainly not for taking the only measures possible to stop a super-villain. Why the authorities went so doggedly after Flash is anyone's guess, but to be fair, there were those who wondered if he could have found a non-lethal way to stop Zoom.

Including Flash himself.

He spent the rest of his days torturing himself with guilt. Despite his flare of rage, Barry clearly had had no intention of snapping Zoom's neck with a desperate chokehold. Barry used to tell me tragic stories of how his fellow officers reacted when they were cornered into using lethal force in the line of duty. No policeman hopes to kill a criminal when he draws his service revolver, but that's part of serving and protecting, and more than ever, Barry wanted to believe that. Had the Flash been an authorized agent of the Central City Police Department, the Zoom case might have begun and ended with an internal affairs investigation, but the CCPD had no provisos for the punishment of unofficially deputized vigilantes.

Thanks to the public sentiment in his favor and due to his ties to the UN-sanctioned Justice League, Flash was allowed a few courtesies. Until such time as his trial commenced, he was released on his own recognizance and allowed to retain his masked identity.

Which was now all he had. Because Barry Allen had never shown up for his wedding, most of the world considered him missing, presumed dead. Under the circumstances, Barry saw no reason to alter that assumption. Should Flash be convicted and sentenced—and he was convinced he might be—Barry would have no choice but to vanish again. Flash was in no hurry to reestablish a life that could be obliterated by the tap of a judge's gavel.

Fiona's fate was even more chilling. The trauma of her own near-death experience, coupled with Barry's disappearance, sent the poor woman spiraling towards madness. Barry missed her terribly, but for her own protection, he was forced to keep his distance. Any sudden shock—including the unexpected appearance of her supposedly dead fiancé—might have sent her over the edge. By the time Barry got his day in court, he no longer knew for certain who his friends were. Several members of the Justice League, though outvoted, called for his expulsion. Wally took the stand as an expert witness and was pressured to speculate, under oath, that there might have been another way to stop Zoom. And Barry's own attorney surprised him with her attempt to explain the passion of the killing by unmasking Flash in court...

...a grandstand stunt that Barry had anticipated. He had his own beautiful face remade by surgeons rather than risk having Fiona haunted by it once it was captured by newspaper photos and television broadcasts.

Worst of all, justice was no longer within his grasp. Abra Kadabra was secretly using his sorcerous powers to unduly influence the jury bent on absolving Barry. A guilty verdict, imprisonment, and public disgrace were certain.

So much had gone wrong so quickly. He'd fallen from dizzying heights into a night-black depth. All his past glories, all his heroic deeds were in danger of being forgotten. He was losing the fight of his life...because he fought alone.

As the trial closed, Barry had only one hope, and that hope lay within one of the jurors.

Deep within.

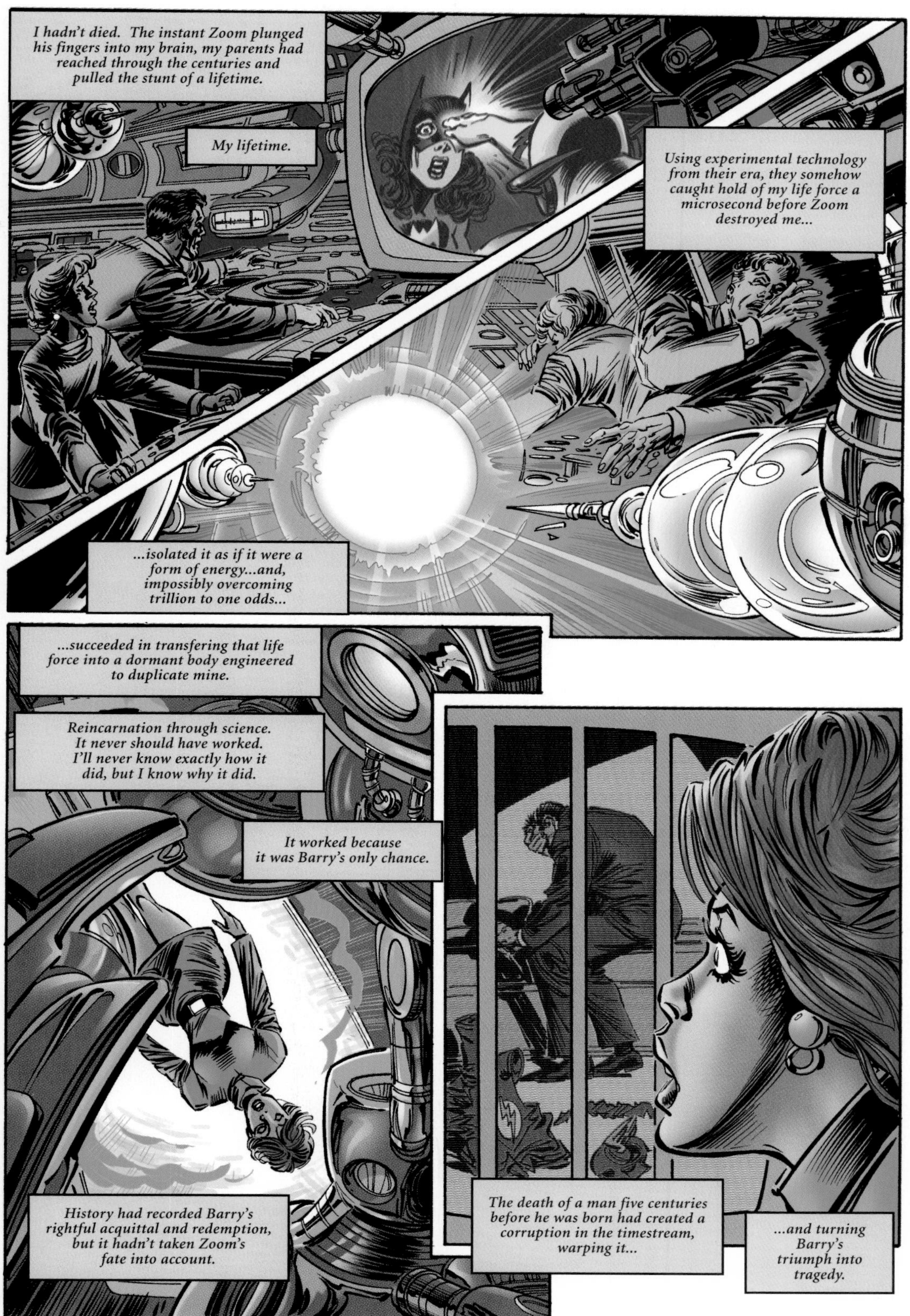
I hadn't died. The instant Zoom plunged his fingers into my brain, my parents had reached through the centuries and pulled the stunt of a lifetime.
My lifetime.
Using experimental technology from their era, they somehow caught hold of my life force a microsecond before Zoom destroyed me...
...isolated it as if it were a form of energy...and, impossibly overcoming trillion to one odds...
...succeeded in transfering that life force into a dormant body engineered to duplicate mine.
Reincarnation through science. It never should have worked. I'll never know exactly how it did, but I know why it did.
It worked because it was Barry's only chance.
History had recorded Barry's rightful acquittal and redemption, but it hadn't taken Zoom's fate into account.
The death of a man five centuries before he was born had created a corruption in the timestream, warping it...
...and turning Barry's triumph into tragedy.

Kadabra knew about this temporal anomaly and vowed to exploit it...but he hadn't counted on my interference.
As a time-traveler familiar both with the challenges of the timestream and the evil of Barry's enemies, it was up to me to outmaneuver Kadabra.
By masquerading as one of the jurors, I was able to help Barry thwart Kadabra's plan...
CENTRAL CITY GAZET
FLASH CLEARED
...and together, we set things right, snatching victory from the jaws of darkest defeat.
Free to go, Barry took care of some final responsibilities...
...AND THAT'S WHY I COULDN'T BE THERE... AND WHY I CAN'T. PLEASE FORGIVE ME, FIONA... AND BE WELL.
...said his goodbyes...
...and started his life over.

Again.

THE SPEED OF LIFE

THERE WAS NO AWKWARDNESS, no shyness. We'd been separated by a thousand years, and it seemed no more than an hour. He told me everything that had happened to him since I'd been gone. Some of it was hard to hear, but to me, it was as if he were speaking of another Barry altogether, and that made it easier to take. What mattered was the here and now...and making up for lost time.

The first order of business was to use reconstructive surgery to restore Barry's good looks, a process easier and more painless in the thirtieth century than a haircut in the twentieth. Barry hemmed and hawed about going through with it, but one plaintive pout got him under the lasers pretty quickly. I still had it.

It was the world's most exotic second honeymoon. We were in an era mostly alien to us, but one so utopian and orderly, one so utterly based on the wonder of scientific progress, Barry couldn't help but warm to it.

Still, somewhere, I heard the ticking of a clock. It wasn't simply a nagging that I hadn't yet told our friends back home that I was still alive, that we were happy. It was a strong sense of time threatening to run out, and I grew resentful over an anxiety that seemed groundless. Barry dismissed my worries with a kiss. He wanted us to focus on the here and now and eased over our only tension.

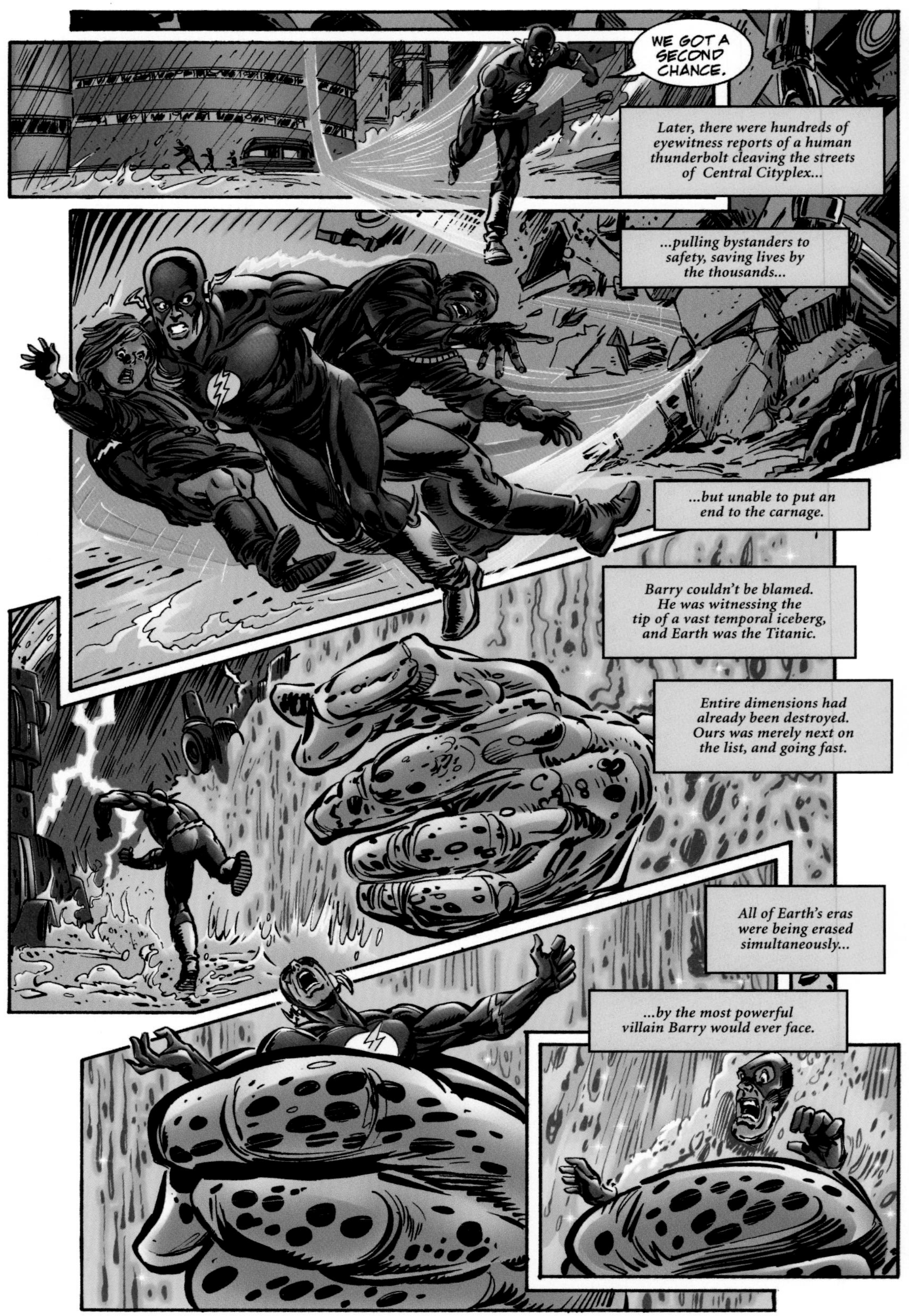
WE GOT A SECOND CHANCE.
Later, there were hundreds of eyewitness reports of a human thunderbolt cleaving the streets of Central Cityplex...
...pulling bystanders to safety, saving lives by the thousands...
...but unable to put an end to the carnage.
Barry couldn't be blamed. He was witnessing the tip of a vast temporal iceberg, and Earth was the Titanic.
Entire dimensions had already been destroyed. Ours was merely next on the list, and going fast.
All of Earth's eras were being erased simultaneously...
...by the most powerful villain Barry would ever face.

RACE TO SAVE THE UNIVERSE

HIS NAME WAS THE ANTI-MONITOR, and he nearly claimed the universe.

His plan was horrifyingly simple and virtually unstoppable. By reaching back in time to the instant of Creation, he planned to remake all reality in his twisted image. In order to defend himself from attack by Earth's heroes, he'd put an entire dark universe to work constructing a cannon powered by antimatter energy.

Barry's vibrational powers were crucial to the Anti-Monitor's scheme; by tapping them, he was allowed free access through all time and space. Severely weakened, but slowly and secretly rebuilding his strength, Barry was held captive in the Anti-Monitor's lair...

Inside the cannon, Barry no doubt stood in awe of its power source. He must have realized he could collapse the antimatter, implode it, but only by reaching a speed beyond any he'd ever achieved.
A speed that would tear him apart.
Did he hesitate? Did the fastest man alive pause, this one, forgivable time?
He knew the Anti-Monitor was on the cusp of victory. Barry knew all of history was depending on what the Flash did next.
Still, he'd spent his life battling the Weather Wizard and the Trickster. A threat this cosmic was almost impossible to comprehend, but maybe possible to run from.
At that moment, he could choose to live or die.
No choice at all.

He pushed himself to the limit and beyond. He always did, to the very end of the race.
I would have expected nothing less of him.
I'll never know what his last thoughts were...
...but I pray they brought him peace.

Without the cannon's protection, the Anti-Monitor fell before the combined might of Earth's super-heroes.
From the Psycho-Pirate, Wally learned about Barry's death and the events that led to it. The tattered, empty costume was proof he needed but didn't want.
When I think back, my heart breaks for Wally. It was his job to carry the news back for all to hear.
DAILY PLANET ARCHIVES
DAILY PLANET
FLASH PERISHES
For all who could hear.
I knew anyway. When Barry left, I did the one thing I swore I'd never do.
I looked up my husband's death.
Barry was gone. I'd never know his love again, not in the way I once had.
The ache in my heart was lessened only by a warmth in my belly.
The growing warmth of life.

CARRYING THE TORCH

TWINS RAN IN THE ALLEN FAMILY. LITERALLY.

I named them Don and Dawn, and they were definitely our children. They inherited my curiosity and their father's speed, and they were a double handful. They turned me gray before my years, and when I look back on all they put me through, all the times I thought they would drive me out of my mind...

...I wouldn't have traded away a day of it. I loved them more with every breath; for the way they were themselves, for the way they were me, and especially for the way they were Barry.

Don was forever studious and timid, Dawn always headstrong and headlong, and I worked hard to give them the sense of belonging and family that I never knew. As adults, they followed their father's example, enjoying a short-lived heroic career as the Tornado Twins, and their adventures deserve a book of their own. Perhaps I'll write it someday, when the wounds have healed; they were murdered while still in their twenties, killed while protecting the Earth from a race called the Dominators.

Dawn married a man named Jeven Ognats, and together they had a girl named Jenni. Jenni manifested super-speed in her early teenage years, used it well, and joined other, equally noble kids as a member of the Legion of Super-Heroes.

My other grandchild led a far more complicated life. Don's son—whose name I cannot divulge for reasons that will soon become clear—was born with super-speed but with no control over his own hypermetabolism. Shortly after birth, he began to age at an insane rate. Earthgov took him in and, in order to keep him emotionally stable, plugged him into a virtual reality that matched his growth. Information, entertainment, entire life scenarios were fed into his mind at super-speed, but nothing stabilized him. At age one, he looked two; at two, he looked twelve. And when I learned that Earth's own president, this youngest Allen's maternal grandfather and a heinous, black soul, was grooming the boy to soon be his super-speed agent of chaos, I kidnapped my grandson and brought him to the 20th century. Soon after, Wally tempered his speed and watched in horror as the hyperkinetic imp adopted a costumed crimefighting identity that fit his personality amazingly well. He called himself Impulse.

Impulse, God bless him, is the poster child for the judgment-impaired. Raised in a virtual world, he's not terribly polished at distinguishing imaginary peril from genuine danger and gleefully jumps giant-feet-first into both with equal aplomb. Worse, he doesn't think; he just does. Wally called it the Single Synapse Theory: from thought to deed in one electric leap, with never a pause to ponder consequence. Wally and Impulse cannot abide one another, and apparently only I realize it's because they're far more alike than either of them would ever admit.

Because Wally would as soon kill Impulse as look at him, we entrusted someone else with his tutoring. Max Mercury, a cool, deliberate, time-hopping hero Wally calls "the zen master of speed," is raising my impatient grandson in the slow Southern town of Manchester, Alabama, and we're all eternally grateful. Like his grandfather before him, the child is blessed with massive amounts of decency and kindness, but it's too easy to forget that when he's barraging you with pointless questions at nine times the speed of sound. I love him dearly, but Max tolerates him.

So far.

All the children were and are heroes, and I couldn't be prouder of any of them. Still, the honor of succeeding Barry fell to the child not ours in blood, but in spirit.
Wally West became the first sidekick ever to fulfill the promise of the role, to take on the identity of his mentor...
...and make it his own.
And while I have studied a thousand years' worth of historical records, Wally continues to surprise me. In his short career as Flash, he's achieved feats that even Barry never matched...
...foremost among them, cracking the secret of the velocity that energizes the Flashes. Barry knew that the human body, however electrified by a freak accident, wasn't capable of producing the speeds they enjoyed.

Sometimes, Barry suspected their power came from elsewhere. By breaking the lightspeed barrier, Wally learned the truth. The speedsters draw their energy from an extradimensional field which lies beyond the speed of light. Neither cognizant nor sentient, it nonetheless serves as a Valhalla to speedsters past, hosting their spirits and using their power wisely, apparently passing it to those it deems worthy.

Wally became the first runner ever to enter the Speed Force and return, in the process becoming the fastest man ever. He has little memory of what he saw while there, so vast and breathtaking was it, but he feels certain of one thing: Barry's a part of it.

EPILOGUE

THE CERTAIN KNOWLEDGE of what tomorrow holds is both a curse and a blessing. Often it takes staggering self-control not to tamper with the lives and destiny of my family, and I try to keep a safe distance. Sometimes, though, the temptation to share in their

joy is too strong to resist...and there is so much wonder in the months and years to come.

I will watch as Wally and Barry share one last great adventure together, a race to infinity that will finally resolve the mysteries that influenced Barry's life and will leave Wally changed forever.

I will stand at Wally's side and help him as best I can through an unexpected, tumultuous marriage, through the marvel of his daughter, and through the tragedy of his son.

I will comfort Impulse when he learns a harsh lesson about life that will cost him a friend but gain him a lifelong companion. I will watch his greatest thrill come in the form of a very special gift from his timelost mother, and I will worry the day his greatest challenge arrives in the form of his own dark twin. There are discoveries to be made in all our lives. Writing this book provided me my most important. I sat at the keyboard for no other reason than to share with the world both what I knew about the husband I so miss and what I knew about heroes. As I wrote, however, I learned a truth of my own, and it will not be soon forgotten. I used to believe that without Barry, I was a lost soul. Now, finally, I realize that his lightning has linked me to a family far more special and wondrous than any I could ever have imagined. I will hold them forever dear. They're almost all I have left.

Almost.